MW00960226

The Wounds That Don't Bleed

Paige Hawk

Copyright © 2019 Paige Hawk

All rights reserved.

This book is entirely fictional. Any characters, names, and occurrences that bear a resemblance to actual individuals living or dead, events, incidents, etc. (except for references to public figures and historical events) are coincidence. Also, the opinions expressed and experiences represented should not be confused with the author's, and not all references may be completely historically accurate. The author is not to be held liable for any actions/reactions that may occur as a result of reading this book.

ISBN: 9781688216655

To those who feel they have no voice...
You do.

CONTENTS

ACKNOWLEDGMENTS

This book wouldn't have been possible without the support of my loved ones and college professors.

In no particular order, a special thanks to:

Mom: We'd be nowhere without you. I love you so much!

Bri: I guess you're all right. Just kidding, you're amazing and gave me the courage to make this happen.

Dad: Thank you for always encouraging me to dream

Sara: Oh Sara, you beautiful baby land mermaid, where would I be without your friendship?! I love you and I like you.

Jen: Your advice made this book 1 million times better. Let's watch *Jeopardy* together and celebrate.

Danny: You made me feel like this was all actually possible; it's one thing to dream, but another to make it happen. I love you.

Suzy and Kate: Your energy and drive are contagious!

Katelyn: You're a fantastic editor and friend! I miss our writing center talks

Aunt Sue and Uncle Brian: You're like having another set of parents; thank you for your love and care.

Claire, Evan, and Victoria: You're genuinely the best cousins anyone could ask for.

Allie and Corey: I'm so happy you guys are now a part of our family!

Aunt Tanya and Uncle Scott: You are kind, caring, adventurous, and I value every memory we make together.

Gram and Pops: Thank you for always wanting what is best for us, and for being the type of grandparents that aren't afraid to have fun

Nanny and Pop Pop: We think of you every day, and aspire to be like you.

Dr. Hinnefeld: You taught me not to look away, and everything else about creative writing.

Dr. Fodrey: You made me feel like my work is worth reading.

Dr. Dougal: You taught me the power of writing.

Meg Mikovits: The writing center helped me become a better writer and editor, but more importantly it was like home. Thank you for crafting that environment!

Dr. Rosen: You encouraged me to be well rounded, bold, and to stay creative.

Everyone in Dr. Hinnefeld's Fiction Writing Class: Your comments and critiques made all the difference.

Trigger Warning

Dear Reader,

This book includes references to drugs, alcohol, rape, self-harm, suicide, violence, sex, etc., in addition to containing language and scenes that may be disturbing to some audiences. While I believe it is important to have open conversations about these things, I know that for some of you, they are too hard to read about.

If you've personally experienced trauma, then on behalf of myself and every other decent human being, I am genuinely sorry. I'm sorry you have been hurt, and I hope that you seek the help you deserve. There are hundreds of organizations dedicated to helping people heal…try asking a friend, family member, counselor, or someone you trust for assistance with finding professional resources.

Peace, Love, Happiness,

Paige Hawk

The Wounds That Don't Bleed

Prologue: August 23rd, 1969

The night wasn't defined by the crocheted blanket with its Charlie
Brown stripes and aroma of burnt leaves. Pat and I had stretched
the blanket across the floor of a classroom so that we could lie on
its scratchy surface the same way we had every Saturday, basking
in the glow of the Christmas lights that we had strung across the
desktops. The glow perfectly illuminated my bleached "Itty Bitty
Titty Committee" tee, something Pat had gifted me on my
nineteenth birthday. We joked that at least this way when guys
stared at my chest, they could read about how they were wasting
their time.

The night wasn't defined by the skipping of the turntable
which refused to play "House of the Rising Sun" despite the stack

of pennies we had taped to the headshell. We added a penny for every missed lyric and kept them there, wearing out records like the tide erodes stone until we each had to pitch in to buy a new one. When we were out of cash we would sneak into the college's radio station to borrow one from the dozens of shelves stacked so tightly, it was a wonder any of the records actually worked. We'd return them after they had become scratched, warped, or grimy as hell. Sometimes they were all three. We loved them so well that whenever one of the school's DJ's attempted to play them, we could recognize that it had once been ours.

The night wasn't defined by the way that our minds melded with the atmosphere, clinging to vibrations that we hadn't known existed —the way the colors of the blanket slowly morphed into one only to slither along the floor and up to the ceiling where it pulsed to the music —No. It's that I had been too distracted by my euphoria to notice Pat trembling by the door, staring blankly at the steel edge of his pocket-knife.

Chapter 1: August 24th, 1968

After getting settled into my dorm and taking a trip to the cafeteria, I sat in my dad's Pontiac licking a cone of strawberry ice cream. He and my mom had reluctantly lent me the car so I could move in to college the same day as everyone else. They didn't want to risk missing Saturday mass; they said something about needing to pray that I'd find God during my college journey, or at least a suitable husband. It never dawned on them that I was going to school to do the opposite.

As I sat in my dad's car, I was surrounded by dozens of other freshmen, all wearing the same wide grins that failed to meet their eyes. The guys were dressed conservatively with chocolate colored trousers and stiff button ups, while the girls wore plaid skirts and asymmetric bobs. The girls who weren't busy saying goodbye to their families toured the campus in packs of three or four, more concerned with scoping out the opposite sex than familiarizing themselves with their classrooms. Taking notice, the guys ribbed each other relentlessly and followed closely behind. Eventually their packs merged into one clump of awkward conversation.

I observed as group after group of clones converged, only stopping when a glob of ice cream spilled onto my top. What wasn't absorbed by its tan fibers dribbled down onto my new jeans.

"Shit," I said, taking a bite from the soggy cone. It tasted like cardboard that had been dipped in wax, so I chucked it out the window. I rummaged through the glove compartment searching for something to wipe up the mess, but only found a copy of the Bible and cigarettes. I threw the Bible onto the car mat but pocketed the smoke pack. Even though I was trying to kick the habit, it felt like a shame to throw them out. Besides, maybe I could barter them like prisoners did. That's all school ever felt like to me anyway. A prison that smelled like chalk dust and furniture polish.

I shoved open the car door and climbed out onto the pavement. A mob of clones paused their conversation in favor of staring at me with the same harsh expression that my mom wore when talking to people who only attended church on Christmas Eve.

I crossed my arms over my chest and bowed my head forward. My hair cascaded around my face, masking my features. My armpits became sacks of perspiration and the warm breeze sent waves of B.O through the air. The girls raised their well-manicured hands to their mouths and whispered to one another as I passed. Removing their sunglasses, they turned to face the men in their group who nodded in my direction.

"Go home you dirty hippie!" they yelled after me. "Friggin' longhair!"

I ran out of the parking lot and across an expanse of freshly mowed grass. I had one goal in mind and one goal only. Get to my dorm: *ASAP*. Sweat dripped down my back as I stopped to plot out the fastest route to my building. I quickly grew frustrated with my brain's inability to process what that might be.

Was it through the nursing building and around the gym?

Dirty Hippie.

Was it cutting across the bursar's office?

Go Home.

I was on the verge of a panicking when I heard the one sound in the world that could calm me: the even strumming of a guitar that had been tuned to an E flat.

I followed the music until I stumbled upon a boy with dishwater hair that grazed his shoulders. He smiled up at me from his seat in the grass and continued playing. I plopped myself down next to him, then hugged my knees towards my chest and listened.

And I tried to tell her that we were the same,

But she left for the city anyway.

Oh she left for the city anyway.

When he finished his song, he unsaddled himself from the Navajo strap of his instrument. Setting it aside, he stretched his legs out in front of him and planted his palms behind him. On his wrists were two woven bracelets that were colorful and handmade. His feet were bare and slightly tanned.

I felt his gaze linger, first on the constellation of freckles on my cheeks, then on the ice cream that had dried and was flaking off like dandruff. I quickly moved to scrape my jeans clean, but he stopped me.

"Leave it," he said, extending his hand.

I extended mine to meet his, but quickly pulled it away. The sweat that was pouring out of it had perfectly preserved the stickiness of the ice-cream.

"I better not," I said pointing to the thick layer of pink slime. I tried wiping it off on the grass, but it didn't help.

He nodded, smiling. "My name's Patrick," he said. "Call me Pat for short."

"Cool name; I named a stray cat that once," I said. Realizing how lame that sounded I added, "I'm June."

He returned to his cross-legged position, retrieved a cigarette from a slouchy backpack, and held it out to me. I shook my head, patting the bulge of the pack that I had in my pocket. He placed the cigarette between his teeth to light it. Once the end of it glowed like newsprint in a fire, he closed his eyes and took a long drag.

"I heard what they called you," he said finally. Smoke streamed from his tobacco stick, filling the space between us. It smelled sweet yet spicy, tempting me. "They're stuck-up puppets of the man. Don't listen to them."

I snorted at the accuracy of his description. "They don't bother you?" I asked.

He shrugged and combed his fingers through his hair. "They called me the same thing earlier. I just gave them the peace sign and kept on walkin'. I feel like if you get mad at them it only spreads the negative vibes."

"I see." I pursed my lips, wishing I could brush the negativity away as easily as he could.

He continued, "It's like...when you're stuck in quicksand, you can't just freak out. You'll only get pulled down faster. Most people are too spazzed to realize you can float in it."

I told him this was a cool way of looking at things, but my chest remained tight. I asked if he could play another song on his guitar and he obliged, choosing "And I Love Her" by The Beatles. He continued to play, choosing songs of all different genres until the sun tucked into the clouds and it began to rain.

Pat hastily stashed his guitar in its smooth black case lined with mustard-yellow velvet, then suggested that we chill together later that evening. I invited him to my dorm, but remembered that we weren't supposed to bring guys there. It was one of the first rules they had included in the orientation packet right below, "Women must wear dresses or skirts with a coordinating blouse to all classes. *No exceptions.*"

"I have an idea," Pat said, interrupting my thoughts. "Let's split for now, but meet up in room 103 of Parker Hall in an hour."

"An hour?" I asked. I was surprised by how quickly he wanted to reconvene, and began calculating whether I'd have time for both showering and figuring out where the hell that building was.

"Yeah, if that's cool with you," he said.

"Okay," I turned to leave but he caught my arm.

"Bring something groovy," he said.

I opened my mouth to ask what he meant, but he said, "See you later," and walked away before I had the chance.

When I entered my room, I was relieved to see that my roommate wasn't there. I hadn't met her yet and knew introductions would take a few minutes, cutting into what little time I had to get ready. I stripped off my clothes and wrapped myself in a towel. There was no way I was going anywhere without rinsing the ice cream and other grossness off my body, even if it meant I'd be a bit late.

It seemed I wasn't the only one who had made a mess of themselves on the first day. I had to wait ten minutes for a shower stall to open up, and when it was finally my turn to go in, the water was ice cold. I swore under my breath as my legs turned purple and web-like beneath the frigid water, but then a thought occurred to me. At least if I froze to death, I wouldn't have to attend school.

When I was finished showering, I slipped into a yellow t-shirt and a pair of jeans with frayed hems. I returned to my room and rummaged through the folder that the school had given me when I first arrived. I quickly discarded a flyer for cheerleading tryouts and continued searching until I found a brochure containing a map. According to the map, Parker Hall was less than a five minute walk from my dorm. Easy-peasy.

I closed the brochure and threw it on my desk which was already overflowing with papers and school supplies from home. I made a mental note to clean it up later. I really didn't want my new roommate to think I was more of a slob than I actually was.

The bell from the school's chapel chimed five times, indicating that it was five o'clock. I quickly grabbed a blanket off of my bed and some Christmas lights that I had draped around its frame earlier. I had no idea whether these counted as being "groovy" but I couldn't arrive empty handed.

It didn't take me long to find Parker Hall. It seemed that a majority of the people on campus had either settled into their dorms for the night or gone out to dinner, so I didn't attract attention like I had earlier. The only person that I came across was a girl wearing a turtleneck and glasses. She didn't bother looking up from her book as I passed. I couldn't help thinking this would've been me if I hadn't made plans with Pat. Alone, digging into a good novel. Maybe after the stressful day that I'd had, that's where I'd end up later.

Each room in Parker Hall was bordered with scratched up blackboards which contrasted against row upon row of shiny laminate desks. When I entered room 103 it was empty except for its furniture, and I was overwhelmed by the scent of mold cohabitating with dust. I wondered when the last time that it received a good cleaning was. Thirty years? Forty? My nose became congested and I sneezed, dropping my belongings on the floor. I cracked open one of three rectangular windows, and used an abandoned textbook to circulate the air. Rain splashed against the ledge of the window, flooding it, but I left it open anyway.

"Did you lay a gasser?" Pat laughed as he entered.

"Don't be an ass," I said putting the book away and turning towards him. My voice was nasally beyond recognition. "It's stuffy as hell in here."

"Yeah it is pretty bad," he said, concerned. "This was just the first room that I thought of. We can try another if you want."

I shook my head. "It's fine. I think having the windows open is really helping."

He nodded and then placed a turntable and an album on one of the desks. I showed him the blanket and the Christmas lights that I had brought along with me. I plugged them into an outlet before wrapping them around several desks that he had pushed to the side of the room. I stretched the blanket in the center of the cocoon that we had created while he moved his turntable to the floor.

When we were finished the room glowed like a jar full of fireflies. The pitter-patter of the rain only added to the cozy vibe, and I began to relax. Pat put on The Mama's and The Papa's, a band that I was familiar with and enjoyed. They were folksy without being cheesy, unlike many of the other popular bands back then. I bobbed my head along to the music while he watched me, a smile playing on his lips. We sat like this for a while just enjoying each other's presence, not bothered by the fact that we had been complete strangers just hours before. Or that, in many ways, we still were.

"So why are you here?" I asked awkwardly.

"What, like on earth? Or at college?" he asked.

"At college," I replied. "You don't seem like the other people around here."

He laughed. "You know, I could say the same about you." He ran his hands up and down his thighs, watching the rain. "My folks said it's either this or the military. I was going to tell them to go to fuck themselves and travel the country, but I didn't want to cut all ties with them. They're good people, even though they don't know a thing about life. I figured I'd miss them eventually."

I nodded and he turned to look at me. It was the first time I noticed just how blue his eyes were, like the sapphire belly-button of a troll doll. Mine were a similar color, but marred with flecks of grey.

"What's your story?" he asked.

I crossed my arms, chilled by the breeze that had picked up outside. "It's not all that different from yours. My parents said I could either go to college to get a husband, or move out and get a job. I decided that college would buy me four more years before I have to enter the real world—maybe five years if I switch majors."

"That's respectable, but why did you choose to go to this college?" he asked. "You do realize it's a Catholic school don't you?"

"You'd have to be an idiot not to," I said, recalling the number of times that the word "Christ" had appeared on the admissions application. It was seven, in case you were wondering. The application had only been two pages.

I continued, "My parents picked out the college and agreed to pay for tuition and everything. Where I went didn't matter to me. I'll be happy so long as I'm away from home with the opportunity to think for myself for a change. I know that a lot of other kids just up and leave when they want that sort of freedom, but I'm not ready to yet."

Pat didn't respond so I continued.

"I think my parents' greatest aspiration is for me to get married, pop out a few kids, then become a stay at home mom. I guess mine is for them to leave me alone."

Pat smoothed the blanket beneath him. Several orange fuzzies clung to his fingers, and he blew them off. "Do you even want to get married?"

I shrugged, surprised that he'd ask such a personal question. Usually people assumed that I wanted a husband, me being a woman and all. Why did he care if I wanted to get married or not?

"I don't know" I said. "Maybe. I can tell you one thing. I don't want the type of my marriage that my parents want for me, and I don't want the type of marriage that most people have. You know the type where the man brings home the bacon and his wife fries it up with a smile. That and I never really thought marriage was much of a possibility for me."

Pat laughed again. It was the type of laugh that didn't beg for attention, but filled the room all the same. I decided that I liked its quiet power, its ability to make me content without trying too hard.

"Well, if you're measuring the likelihood of you finding a husband based upon the soshes that attend our school, then I'd say your chances are pretty slim.'"

"Sadly I couldn't agree more."

The record began to skip, so Pat removed his wallet from his back pocket. He took out three pennies and stacked them on the headshell of the turntable, but they immediately toppled off. He put one of them back onto it and commented that next time he'd have to remember to bring along tape. Preventing records from skipping was usually a three-penny type of job, but he could only stack one penny before gravity took over. He said he was surprised that the record player had gone this long without interruption. Usually it skipped by song two.

"So what are you studying?" I asked when there was a lull in the conversation.

"History," he said. "You?"

"Same. Please tell me you're taking Level I American History with Professor Hodge. I heard he's a huge dick."

"Who told you that?" he asked.

"My cousin. She graduated from here a few years ago. She didn't use those exact words but that's what I got out of the conversation."

Pat arched his eyebrow. "Yeah I have him. I'll bet that you have Intro to European History with Dr. Anders too."

"How'd you guess that?" I asked.

"I think there are so few history classes offered that we *have* to take the same ones. It isn't exactly a popular major you know."

I nodded. "Yeah that's probably true. But what are the chances that the school's only hippies would both choose the same major?"

Pat scratched behind his ear then flicked dry skin off of his fingers. I pretended not to notice.

"Well I'd say the chances were pretty good," he said. "What else would we have studied? Home Economics? Business? Theology? Nah, none of that would make sense for us. It's all too normal and there's not enough freedom. Besides, I wanna change the world and history is going to help me." He drew himself up as though this was something he was proud of.

I was surprised by this. He didn't come across as an overly confident dude, and because he had been slouching from the moment I met him, I didn't think that he was capable of such good posture. I looked at him attentively and gestured for him to continue. When he didn't I asked, "How so?"

He stood up and walked over to the window. He gazed out of it for several minutes with his hands pressed firmly against the frame. He said, "I want to achieve peace, and not just the superficial peace that we have when we aren't at war. I mean real peace. The type where everyone is so happy with their own lives that they quit judging others by how they live theirs or by what they look like. I want everyone to know...No.... Not know. *Understand* that violence is a shit way to deal with their problems...

"I figure that history is just a collection of conflicts that were usually resolved through bad tactics. By studying the means and the ends I know I can come up with some sort of a better solution, some way to do what's never been done. If not then I'll at least know what not to do, and that's a start."

I stared at him in awe, and a wave of nausea overcame me. I thought of how here, standing in front of me, was one of the most empathetic individuals to walk this earth. What turned my stomach was knowing that no one else would look at him the same way. They'd see his lengthy hair and far-out clothes and assume that he was stupid or on drugs, or both. If he was lucky they'd write him off as some fantasyland lunatic that wasn't worth listening to. If he wasn't lucky, they'd bully him like they'd bullied me as soon as I had stepped out of my car. Maybe they'd treat him worse since he was a guy.

"Are you alright?" he asked. "You look like you're going to barf."

"Yeah I'm fine," I lied. "I'm just hungry."

He nodded and extended his hand out to meet mine. I took it and he helped me up off the floor. I thought about how good our hands felt when they were together, and hesitated to pull away. A part of me hoped he was thinking the same thing.

"Wanna get something to eat?" he asked. "There aren't a heck of a lot of good places in town, but there's a new restaurant I wanted to try. I think it's one of the few places that have a vegetarian option other than salad."

"That sounds good," I said a little too quickly.

"Are you sure?"

I closed my eyes, willing my stomach to settle down. "Mhmm. I'm looking forward to it."

"Great."

We gathered our belongings and left Parker Hall, one optimist looking to change the world, and me just trying to get by in it.

Chapter 2: August 26th, 1968

My alarm clock went off, so I swiped it onto the floor. It landed with a dramatic crash but the damn thing kept going. I rubbed my eyelids then slapped my cheeks for good measure. Waking up had never been my forte. At home my mom used to barge into my room and shout at me that it was time to get up. If I refused to rise, she'd come in with a spray bottle full of ice water and spritz me like a dog. I'd do my best Chihuahua impression, and she'd get frazzled.

"Oh honestly, Juniper!" she'd cry. "Can't you get up without waking the neighbors? They're beginning to talk!"

I'd continue to bark until she left me alone.

My roommate popped her head out of her blanket burrito and groaned. "Are you going to get that? I don't have to be up for another hour."

"Yeah... Sorry." I rolled out of bed and turned the alarm off, taking the sheets with me. I set the clock back on the side table, silently cursing it for doing its job a little too well. Couldn't it have cut me some slack on my first day of classes?

It was only our second morning together and I could already tell my roommate didn't like me. I can't say that I blamed her. The first night after grabbing dinner with Pat, I snuck in at three a.m., about four hours after curfew. The previous night I came in at midnight, nearly giving her a heart attack because of my clumsy entrance.

Sneaking in wasn't nearly as difficult as I had expected. On the first night once I realized that Pat and I would be staying out late, I introduced myself to the quiet book nerd who I had passed on my way to Parker Hall. I told her that I'd pay her seventy-five cents a week if she'd sign my name in the dorm log on the weekends. At first she was hesitant, worried that she might get caught. I assured her that the Head Residents didn't actually care who signed the book as long as there was a signature for each person by the end of the night. My cousin told me so herself. She had said disapprovingly, "Those Head Residents barely pay attention to anything that goes on around there. I even saw a group of boys sneak in once."

Once the log was signed and the dormitory doors locked for the night, all I had to do was climb in through my window. It was one of the perks of living on the first floor, along with only having to climb one flight of stairs. Easy in, easy out, as long as my roommate didn't squeal on me. Given that she had several bottles of vodka stashed beneath her bed, I wasn't too worried. If she reported me, I'd report her, and she knew it. Nothing could get you expelled from school faster than staying out with a boy after curfew. But nothing ruins the reputation of church mouse faster than a bottle of liquid sin. My roommate was someone with more rosaries than all of Vatican City, so reputation meant a lot to her.

Unlike me, Pat didn't have to sneak in if we stayed out late. While girls were expected to be Virgin Mary, guys didn't even have a curfew. They were still expected to sign in and out, but only so that the Head Resident could keep track of their whereabouts in case of emergency. Other than that, they operated on the honor

system and were protected by the mindset that "boys will be boys."

When I arrived at Parker Hall it was bustling with other

students all trying to find their classes. One of these students was a

fidgety guy with coke-bottle glasses and a silver key tied around

his neck. Compared to this guy, I had nothing to be nervous about.

It didn't matter that we were all college kids and supposedly

adults. There was a high chance someone would tie him to the

flagpole by the end of the day, or at least steal his glasses.

Sure enough, a jock came up behind him and slapped him

on the back. "Hey nerd. Where's your spacecraft?" he jeered as he

passed.

The kid nearly fell over from the impact of the blow, and

the books that he was carrying slid out of his arms. The bully

became distracted by a tall blonde with tangerine skin, and

whistled at her. She flashed him a grin and he took this as his cue

to pursue her.

As the kid with the glasses knelt down to retrieve his books, I rushed over to help.

"Are you okay?" I asked. "That guy hit you pretty hard."

He looked at me like I was termite. "I'm just peachy. Now would you leave me alone already? If people see me with a longhair, I'm doomed. They already hate me."

Nice, I thought. *Even the nerds don't want to associate with me.*

I stood up, trying not to look as insulted as I felt. "Oh. Yeah, of course. Sorry. I hope you have a good day."

He shook his head dismissively and scurried out of sight.

"Asshole," I muttered once he was long gone. I only wished I had said it to his face.

☼☺☼

I easily found my class because it was located in room 103, the same one that Pat and I had hung out in two days prior. When I entered I was surprised to see that Pat was already there. He waved me down, having saved the desk next to him for me. It was on the left side of the room, right next to the window. He told me he had already cracked open the window to disperse the stale air. He knew how bad my allergies were, and didn't want me feeling like crap on day one. I thanked him and settled into my seat, taking a look around.

We were surrounded by people in crisp shirts and shoes so shiny they doubled as a mirror. I was one of only three girls in the room. The other two were behind me, whispering to one another. Their words were too muffled to make out, no matter how hard I tried to eavesdrop. I instinctively knew that they were gossiping about me.

"Ignore them," Pat mouthed.

I took a deep breath and tugged at the sleeve of my dress.

"Hey," Pat said, poking me so that I'd look up. "I'm serious. Forget them."

I may not have been able to hear what they were saying, but I had a feeling that he could. Whatever it was, it clearly wasn't good. I pulled out my textbook and tried reading it as a distraction, but it only made me sleepy. I ended up studying the scratches on the chalkboard instead.

Professor Hodge strode in with his hands in his pockets and a notable air of confidence. I was never so glad to see a professor in all my life. He traced his clean shaven face with his thumb and forefinger, sizing us all up. His eyes lingered on Pat and me longer than everyone else, and I slid down further in my seat. Pat cracked a smile in my direction and shook his head.

After several minutes of silence, Professor Hodge leaned against the edge of his desk and crossed his arms. The wood groaned beneath his weight. "This is American History I," he began. "If you think that this will be an easy A, then you might as well leave now. If you think that I will tolerate cheating, note passing, or any of that other juvenile garbage, you are wrong. You are adults and I will treat you as such. You will be graded according to the grade that you earn, and nothing more. Rarely do I give A's. Additionally, I will not tolerate tardiness of assignments nor late entrance into my class. Is that clear?"

The class's response was divided between fear, respect, and annoyance. Several kids took his advice and left.

"Good." He went over to the door and locked it with a swift *click*.

The kid in front of me eyed the exit as though he wished he had taken it while he still had the chance. I had the sudden urge to use the restroom, but knew better than to raise my hand and ask.

Pat clenched his fists like he was grasping steel bars. He searched his pockets for a pencil and withdrew a piece of paper from his notebook. In it he scribbled, "Stone walls do not a prison make, nor iron walls a cage." I prayed that Professor Hodge wouldn't see what he had written. He didn't seem like the type of guy that would appreciate poetry.

The proceeding lecture was boring at best, and I struggled to read the chalkboard once my eyes glazed over from fatigue. I began to wonder why I had chosen history as my major, and whether or not all of my classes would be this dull. At one point I tried counting the days left until graduation, but I wasn't great at math. I just knew the sum was something ridiculously far off, which made the lecture feel even longer.

Pat, on the other hand, was genuinely enjoying himself. His pencil raced from left to right as he took copious notes. I didn't know whether he was writing down what the professor was saying verbatim or filling the book with his own thoughts. His writing had become too tightly scrawled to see. All that I knew was that if he kept this up, he'd need new school supplies by next week.

The only time that he stopped writing was to ask questions of Hodge or to learn more about the ideologies behind what he was teaching. At first I thought that this would get him kicked out of class, but Hodge seemed to like having an excuse to show off his knowledge. The other students were less charmed, and took to eye rolling and wishing that Pat would just shut up already. He was earning himself the reputation as teacher's pet. This wasn't a good reputation for anyone to acquire, let alone someone who was already an outcast.

When the bell from the chapel announced that class was over, Pat and I were the last to leave. Professor Hodge stopped us as we were crossing through the threshold.

"You know, I never thought that I'd have two hippies in my class. Isn't attending college the opposite of 'sticking it to the man?'" His tone oozed smugness and my cheeks burned crimson.

Pat turned to face Hodge, his expression perfectly calm. Looking him straight in the eyes he said, "Sticking it to the man doesn't mean that you have to avoid all of his institutions. It's about living how you want to regardless of them. I have my reasons for being here, and so does she," he pointed to me, "And those reasons demand respect."

Professor Hodge looked taken aback. Clearly he hadn't expected such an articulate response, even after Pat had proven his intelligence in class. He hesitated a moment before responding, "You might be surprised to learn that I actually do respect you and Ms. Carter. History is made by those who see beyond the paradigm and challenge it. I may not understand hippies nor agree with your beliefs, but that doesn't mean that I don't respect you."

Pat opened his mouth to speak but Hodge continued. "Do not think that you can use your identities as an excuse not to turn in your papers or sit for examinations. I expect the same level of studiousness from you two as I do from everyone else who walks through my door. Rules *will* be followed." His tone lightened up significantly. "How you go about completing these assignments is entirely up to you, though I do recommend you be careful. I am, as it is well known, a tough grader." He waved us away with the newspaper he was clutching. "Now leave before you're late for your next class. I never provide tardy notes."

Once Pat and I were out in the hallway we exchanged confused glances.

"Does that mean that he actually *likes* us?" I asked, my cheeks returning to their usual pale shade.

"I doubt it. Like and respect are two different things, and I'm not sure whether he is capable of liking anything outside of himself," Pat said.

We laughed as we continued down the hallway and to our next class, unable to shake our shock at what had just happened, nor our newfound admiration of the college's least popular professor.

Chapter 3: August 30th, 1968

By the first Friday of the semester, I was really, *really* tired.

Adjusting to new classes and a new living situation is hard enough

for anyone, let alone someone who doesn't fit in. I was surprised

by how immature everyone on campus was. By the way that they

poked fun at me, you'd have thought that I was a giraffe with a

perm and rainbow stripes, or an alligator on roller blades.

It's true that we didn't have a lot in common. They liked

partying and had little interest in expanding their knowledge and

beliefs beyond what had already been ingrained in them. The boys'

main goal was to earn their Mrs. The girls were only there for their

Mr.

I, on the other hand, was there to earn a real degree. I preferred chilling out alone in my dorm or elsewhere with Pat, and was hungry to discover more about who I was and what I really wanted from life. I didn't expect the clones to understand this. That would've been asking too much of them. But I had hoped that they'd at least leave me be.

☼☺☼

When classes were over I headed back to my dorm for a much needed nap. I passed by the Head Resident who was busy reading a glossy magazine. On its cover was a rail thin woman with cropped hair and doe eyes. Her lower lashes were individually defined with black mascara, making her look modern but a little creepy. I wondered how many girls around campus would be bold enough to try such a strange, doll-like look. I decided that none of them would.

The Head Resident looked up at me so I attempted a weak smile.

"It's June, right?" she asked, already bored with the conversation.

"Yep. That's me."

She glanced at the shiny black phone on her desk. "Your mother called. She wants you to return it as soon as you can. She said to tell you it's important."

I groaned. So much for my nap. "Thanks," I said, heading to the student lounge.

We weren't allowed phones inside of our rooms, but there were several call stations there. All of them were already in use, so I sat on one of the couches and waited. It was a stiff old thing coated with crumbs, nail polish, and a flaky white substance. I scraped off some of this gunk while observing the people on the phones.

The girl on the corner phone was biting her nails, rocking back and forth in her chair. The girl next to her was chatting with someone who I guessed was her boyfriend, judging by her effortless flirting. The third girl was poker-faced, and held the phone with a vice grip. "Mhmm. Mhmm. Yes," She mumbled. "Mhmmm. Yeah. Alright. I promise. See you later." She clicked the phone onto its receiver and walked away coldly.

I took her place at the call station and dialed my mom. The handset was slick from sweat so I wiped it clean with a tissue. I held it as far away from my face as possible without hindering my ability to hear. Even at a distance, it smelled faintly of mint gum. I wrinkled my nose.

"Hello. You've reached the Carter residence. Mrs. Carter speaking," my mom said in her most polite voice possible. Her voice was almost always formal when she first picked up, as though the first lady might be on the line.

"Hey mom."

"Juniper!" she exclaimed. "Hang on a second dear; just let me finish folding these socks."

I imagined her sitting on her neatly made bed, carefully tending to each individual sock, bra, and pair of underwear. For her, laundry was serious business, but also a pleasure. Her folding was Olympic quality, and she was the only person I knew who had tried every brand of detergent in existence, sometimes traveling out of town to get her hands on something new she saw advertised on the TV.

"Alright I can talk now," she said, sliding a drawer shut. "I'm so glad you called."

"You asked me to," I said. "You told the Head Resident that it was important."

She ignored me and rattled on. "How was your first week of school? Have you made any friends? Are there any cute boys? Of course it doesn't matter how cute they are if they don't attend church regularly or if they're studying something silly like history or—"

"It was ok," I interrupted.

"Just okay? Oh Juniper, please tell me you're at least putting an effort into making a good impression. Have you tried smiling?"

"Smiling?"

"Yes, you know... If you see someone who looks friendly, give them a smile. You have such nice cheekbones, and your teeth aren't too crooked. I was reading in a magazine that men prefer women who look happy, and eager to please. Do you feel you look happy and eager to please?"

I rolled my eyes, glad that she couldn't see me. Doing this had earned me an hour long lecture on more than one occasion. "Mom, can we talk about something else? Please?"

She huffed. "I'm only saying it doesn't hurt to try a little harder. By the way that you act, I sometimes wonder if you're *determined* not to find a husband."

And sometimes I wondered if she was disappointed that I was her daughter. But I was getting over it. Would she?

I tried to change the subject. "So how have you been mom? Did anything exciting happen this week?"

She immediately cheered up. "Well, Ms. Nelle came over and asked me whether I could get a cherry stain out of her apron. It took a little elbow grease, but by the time I was through with it, it looked brand new. She was so grateful that she baked me a cake. You would have loved it June, it was lemon with raspberry jam and buttercream. She canned the jam herself just a couple of weeks ago. Actually, if you'd like I can freeze you a piece. There are still a couple left."

I had grown bored with our conversation and started eavesdropping on the one going on two chairs down. The girl was now shouting that she hated college into the receiver, while pounding her fist against the wooden divider. The whole row of tables shook from the impact, and a pencil rolled off of the one next to me. The girl who had been flirting shot her a dirty look.

"Goodness, what is all that noise?" My mom asked. "Where are you calling from? A construction site?"

I cringed at her attempt at a joke. "It's nothing. I think someone is just having trouble adjusting to college life."

"I see." She was silent for several minutes, so I assumed she had gone back to folding laundry.

"Well honey, if you ever get overwhelmed with school you can always come home. There's no need for a girl as pretty as you to go to college. I bet your father could get you a job in his office. How are you at answering phones?" she paused mulling it over. "Well it doesn't really matter how good you are at it. I'm sure they'll train you. We'll just have to figure out what to do with that hair of yours. You can't go off to work with it looking the way it did before you left for school—like a Sasquatch or something. Do you even bother brushing it?"

My roommate appeared behind me and tapped me on the shoulder. She asked, "Are you almost done?" and pointed to her watch.

"Yeah just a sec," I whispered.

"What was that dear?" my mom asked. "Did you say something?"

"Uh, mom, I have to go. Other people want to use the phone."

My roommate gave me a thumbs up.

I returned the gesture, glad to have a legitimate reason to hang up.

"Alright dear, I don't want to hold them up. I love you and I miss you."

"Bye mom. I love you too."

"Don't forget to smile."

"I'll try not to."

I had barely finished talking when the phone was ripped out of my hand. Ordinarily I'd have been pissed, but I wasn't in a foul mood. Actually, talking to my mom had been sort of nice. She had managed to offend me in almost every way possible, but instead of bringing me down it had inspired me. Suddenly I was more determined than ever to stay in college, if only to avoid becoming a secretary at my dad's office. It wasn't that I didn't respect secretaries. As far as I was concerned, they were the unsung heroes of every workplace. I just figured I'd be fired the first time someone asked me to make them a cup of coffee and I responded, "You have two hands. Make it your fucking self."

Re-energized by the conversation with my mom, I dropped my books off at my room and went outside. The stale air of the student lounge was toxic compared to the air out there. I allowed it to fill my lungs completely, smiling as I exhaled. My mom would have been proud of how pretty I looked just then. I threw my head back to look at the clouds, and spread my arms out like wings. I spun around and around as the breeze picked up, dancing with me. I imagined that I was a dove, flying above the trees, peering down at all of the people below. They looked so small and unimportant at such great heights. Like specks of pepper on a Caesar salad.

"Hey June," Pat called, striding towards me.

I closed my eyes and continued my strange choreography. I wasn't ready to come down to earth just yet, and I hadn't completely registered his presence.

Pat stood patiently across from me, watching me without judgment. Several leaves were shaken loose from a nearby tree and tickled my cheeks as they floated downward, landing in my hair and eventually on the grass. I opened my eyes and gazed down at the small pile that had collected at my feet. I then looked at Pat and blushed, suddenly embarrassed by my abnormal behavior.

Picking up on this he said, "It's a great day to be alive isn't it? Makes me wish I were a bird so I could fly around for a while." He mimicked the way I had outstretched my limbs and twirled once.

I no longer felt silly. "Yeah it's pretty nice out here," I said. "What are you up to?"

He shrugged. "Just bumming around. I thought maybe I'd borrow an album from the radio station for tomorrow."

"What's tomorrow?"

"Saturday. I was hoping we could hang out again in Parker Hall. Maybe make it a weekly occurrence. You dig?"

I didn't have anything better to do, so I nodded. "Yeah I'd like that."

He told me that the radio station was headquartered in the library, so we set off towards it. I asked him how this was logical, given that libraries are known for their silence. He said that the station was in the basement, out of sight and out of mind. No one could hear anything that went on down there.

"I didn't know that you could borrow albums from the radio station," I said when we were nearly there. "That's awesome. I'm going to do it all the time, as long as their taste isn't too lame."

He bit his lower lip. "Surprisingly they have a good collection. But they don't let just anyone borrow them."

I stopped walking. "What, do you know someone who runs it?"

His face twisted into a devious expression. I half expected a thorny tail to come poking out of his pants. "No. But I know when its empty and I'm pretty good with locks."

"Works for me," I said.

We entered the library which was eerily quiet. Since it was a Friday afternoon, most people were getting dolled up to go partying, or packing to go home. If Pat hadn't been around, I may have done the latter. As much as I valued the sense of freedom that came with being out on my own, I would've done anything for a home-cooked meal and my own bed. Also, I kind of missed the smell of my dad's coffee brewing in the morning, and the incessant whining of the vacuum as my mom cleaned.

Pat led me to a heavy brown door at the end of a long hallway. The hinges whined as he pushed it open. On the other side of it was a wrought-iron stairwell that we quickly descended. When we reached the bottom, we found ourselves in another long hallway containing two restrooms, a closet, and the radio station. On the station's door was a schedule indicating people's shifts.

Pat pointed to it. "See, told you it's empty," he said.

I folded my arms. "*That's* how you know it's empty? Here I was thinking you had psychic powers or something. Anyone can read a sign."

"Sorry to disappoint," he said jokingly. "I only use my psychic powers on Tuesdays."

"Very funny," I said reaching for the doorknob. I twisted it, but it refused to budge.

"Here, let me get that," he said, searching his pockets. He pulled out two bobby pins, one of which he unbent into a straight line. He tucked his hair behind his ears and knelt down by the lock. He stuck the straight pin in first, then the other, and got to work. He reminded me of a surgeon, or my dad when he fiddled with technology. In no time we heard a click, and the door easily opened.

"After you," he said, sliding the pins back into his jeans.

"Now I'm impressed," I said flipping on the lights. "Do I want to know how you got so good at picking locks?"

"Probably not," he said, looking down at the carpet. It was plush and littered with paper, as though someone had forgotten where the trash can was. I picked up a piece and read it; it was a list of songs which had been crossed out and re-arranged numerous times, then crumpled into a ball. I threw it away but Pat pulled it out of the bin and returned it to the floor.

"We should touch as little as possible," he said. "We don't want anyone to know we were here."

"You're right. I'm Sorry." I sucked at being sneaky.

The radio station was no bigger than an average bedroom, but boy was it a sight to see. It was lined with several red shelving units which were stacked top to bottom with records. Pulling out albums from the heap was like trying to tear a bear cub away from its mom: difficult and not recommended. The shelves shook as we poured through their contents, threatening to topple over. Pat held them down as I looked, and I did the same for him, neither one of us wanting the other to be flattened into a human pancake.

As we took stock of the collection I wondered where the albums had come from. Had they been donated? Purchased? Accidentally left behind and then nabbed? I no longer felt guilty for borrowing from this stash. They had enough music to get by without an album or two. I wasn't even sure anyone listened to the college radio.

Pat pulled an album by The Byrds. I pulled one by my favorite group, Simon and Garfunkel. He raised an eyebrow.

"What? Not a fan?" I asked.

He took the album from me and perused the track list. "I never gave them much of a chance," he admitted, "but they might be good."

"Never gave them a chance?" I asked. "Why the hell not?"

He shrugged. "I heard their first album, and it wasn't anything special. It was way too acoustic, even for me, and didn't have enough soul." My face fell and he added, "But I'm looking forward to hearing how they've progressed since then. If you like them, then they must be cool."

I sighed. "A lot of people didn't like their first album, but you might like them now. What I really love about their songs is the lyrics. They're like poetry suspended in sound."

"Poetry suspended in sound," he repeated. "I like that. Maybe you should write songs."

"I'm not much of a writer," I said.

He handed the album back to me. I hugged it, thinking how similar it was to my chest. Flat.

"I bet you can write better than most people," he said.

"True. But I don't really enjoy writing and it doesn't come easy to me. Take that essay that Hodge assigned on the second day of class. How long did it take you to complete?"

His forehead wrinkled. "I don't know. Maybe half an hour?"

"Half an hour? Are you serious?"

He nodded. "Yeah. Forty-five minutes tops."

"Jesus Pat, I was thinking it took most people an hour or two to complete. You know how long it took me? The whole damn night, that's how long."

He touched my shoulder consolingly. "No one can be good at everything," he said. "If you don't like to write, then what do you do for fun?"

I took a moment to consider this. Neither my parents nor my friends in high school had ever asked me such a question. None of them had cared enough to.

"I like drawing and painting," I said at last. "I can't do anything realistic, although I wish that I could. I'd kill to be able to do portraits. I mainly do abstract pieces that no one ever understands. My mom says that they're ugly and a waste of time."

He scratched the stubble on his chin. "I'm sure they're anything but ugly."

I shrugged. "It's hard to tell. I think they're decent. But art without subjectivity isn't art at all."

"I guess not," he said, cocking his head. "If you like art so much, then why are you studying history?"

"I like history too," I said.

"Oh come on, June. I could tell by the end of our first class together that you've already checked out. You're not passionate about history like I am, and that's ok. But it's going to be a long four years if you keep pretending you are."

I rubbed my ears which had begun to burn. "Being a history major makes sense, that's all," I said. "My parents flipped when they found out I'm taking art as one of my electives. They'd probably disown me if I became an artist."

"If you say so."

He turned and ran his index finger along the stacks. He pulled another album and laughed. "You have to see this," he said, flinging it at me like a Frisbee. It rebounded off of the album that I was already holding and slid across the floor.

I picked it up and snorted. On its cover were three women with hair as round as beach balls, matching robin-egg pullovers, and awkward half-smiles. Their group was called The Faith Tones, with the track title "Jesus Use Me" displayed in pink letters. It was the most worn album we had come across, with dozens of greasy fingerprints and scratches.

"If I ever look anything like these women, please shoot me," I said.

He gave me a once over. "I don't think you could look like them if you tried. For one you're much prettier, for another you've got style."

I ignored his compliments, unsure of what to say. "We have to borrow it," I teased. "I bet it cracks the list of top 100 albums of all times."

"I would love to," Pat said sarcastically. "Sadly it appears as though it is the one album they'll notice is gone."

"Damn. I really thought it'd be groovy," I said sliding it back in the stacks. "I guess we should just stick with our other selections then."

"What a shame."

After a long laugh, we agreed that it was time to go. We had been there almost an hour, and hadn't coordinated an alibi if we were to get caught. We left the station unseen, and the library as well. Pat took the albums back to his dorm for safekeeping, and came out grinning. Mission accomplished.

We spent the rest of the day walking around together, not doing much of anything, but not ready to leave each other's company. An unspoken yet mutual understanding had formed; an understanding that we'd be each other's shadow, keeping each other from experiencing the sting of loneliness, without the awkwardness that comes with getting to know someone. In other words, together, he and I would simply *be*.

Chapter 4: September 27th, 1968

A little over a month into school, Professor Hodge had already

distributed two tests and six essays. I received a "C" on both

exams and was as disappointed by the low marks as I was relieved.

The questions he asked were intentionally tricky and the essays

practically required a PhD. I had tried talking to him after class to

see what I could do to improve my grades, but all he ever said was

that my work lacked inspiration, whatever that meant. I quickly

learned to be satisfied with my average grades in his class. All I

could do was do my best.

Pat was doing annoyingly well. He was the only person in

the class to earn an "A" on all assignments, a fact that Professor

Hodge made well known. It didn't help him shake his reputation as teacher's pet, but I was amazed by how smart he was. Not once had I seen him study outside of class, and when I took a closer look at his notebook, it was full of his own personal reflections rather than notes.

The other kids weren't nearly as impressed by his intellect. They took to accusing him of cheating and stole his textbooks when he wasn't looking. If they weren't strewn about the classroom they were usually in one of the building's trash cans. As he struggled to retrieve them, students walked by and made comments such as "Oh look, a longhair in his natural habitat" or "So that's where his stench comes from. Take a bath already, won't ya?"

Pat didn't seem to hear them and continued to excel, even earning himself a job offer as a tutor in the academic support center. He turned it down claiming that he couldn't bear to be surrounded by his peers more than he had to be. But I could tell through his cool exterior that he was honored to have been asked.

The project that had earned him the offer was an essay and a presentation regarding our standpoint on the Vietnam War. Hodge said that he usually steered clear of modern problems but the deans had forced him to assign this project. It was the school's way of trying to prevent student protests that could bring negative media attention. The theory was that by giving students the chance to voice their political opinions academically, they wouldn't feel the need to stage an actual protest. My theory was that this logic was as sound as abstinence only sex education courses. If you're going to do it, you're going to do it. No amount of schooling is going to squelch the urge.

On the day that the project was due, I was the first person forced to present. I walked to the front of the room ignoring the whispers about my flowy skirt and trembling hands. One person stuck out their foot in an attempt to trip me, but I dodged it. Pat held up a peace sign and a sheepish smile that said "You got this."

In a way, he was right. Within minutes I had managed to bore my classmates into a stupor that rendered them too tired to take a crack at my argument. Pat was the only one that remained alert the entire time that I was up there and, as I was sliding back into my desk, he congratulated me for not passing out. I barely had enough time to stick my tongue out at Pat before Professor Hodge announced that it was his turn to take the floor.

Pat got up from his chair causing it to creak loudly. He walked to the back of the room slowly but with his head held high. I had no idea what he was up to, but I knew something special was about to happen. I could tell by the way that the energy in the room was shifting from lethargic to alert.

"I believe that the front of the room is *this* way," Professor Hodge sneered.

Pat ignored him and continued to the far left corner where a black case was leaning against the wall. He carefully unclasped the gold latches and lifted his guitar up over his head with one graceful motion. The class became too curious to mock him, and watched silently as he dragged a chair in front of the chalkboard. They didn't cringe as the legs scraped against the floor with an ear piercing screech, nor while he adjusted his strings. Goose pimples sprang up on my arms and legs.

He began with an open D chord and strummed several times before switching to a G major and then back to D again. The resulting sound was bright and pleasant, yet laced with a sense of sorrow which was augmented by somber lyrics.

He sang:

I stare at the sunset; the orange warms my soul,

I remember the children across the globe.

They run under cover, the color deforms,

They stumble on mines and are gone.

We send off our brothers to please Uncle Sam,

For our lives he don't give a damn.

We're fighting for freedom but freedom demands,

We stand up for ourselves and give others a chance.

The song continued through several verses before slowly fading out. When he was done playing and the last note resonated, the only other sound that could be heard was sniffling. Pat returned his instrument to its case and hesitantly the class began to clap. I could tell by their mixed expressions that their minds were struggling to process what they had just heard. Was Pat the coolest guy in school for singing better than Paul McCartney? Or did his talent make him even more of an outcast?

Professor Hodge interrupted their thoughts. "Well that was fascinating. Thank you for that creative interpretation of the assignment. I believe you have just earned yourself yet another 'A'. It must be some sort of a record. Is anyone brave enough to follow that act? "

Nobody was, so Hodge called on a cheerleader whose presentation was so boring, I instantly fell asleep. Even Pat didn't pretend to be interested, writing poetry on his desktop instead.

Once class was dismissed, Pat grabbed his guitar and we headed outside. The next class on our schedules had been cancelled, leaving us with a whole afternoon to relax while drinking in the cool autumn air. We settled on a patch of grass beneath a fiery tree, and then I listened to him play as I had so many times before.

I was mesmerized by his calloused fingers as he tenderly stroked the strings, so rough and yet so beautiful. I was mesmerized by the way that his lips turned slightly upwards as he sang, and how his eyes crinkled at the corners when he looked at me.

"Hey Pat," I asked when he finished his first song, "have you ever considered being a musician?"

"Well," he said, "I play guitar and I sing. Doesn't that qualify me as one?" Sarcasm oozed from his voice like maple syrup

"Yeah, but I meant professionally. I think you could make it big if you tried."

Pat tilted his head. "I thought about it. But money and fame are two monkeys that I don't want on my back. I'm satisfied playing the way I do; sitting on the grass with the coolest chick in the world," his gaze shifted away from me, "and playing in my dorm driving the other dudes crazy."

He began playing again before I had time to respond, and continued up until he was too hungry to continue. He asked me to lunch as he did every day, and I said, "Sure. Just give me a second to get changed. It's getting chillier by the minute."

He walked me to my dorm and waited outside of the building. Even though nobody was around, we didn't feel like bending the "No boys allowed" rule.

I entered the hallway leading to my room and was alarmed to see that my door was wide open. *Maybe I forgot to shut it,* I thought, trying to calm my mounting anxiety. *Or maybe my roommate's class got cancelled too, and she's in there just*

hanging out.

What little peace of mind I had mustered quickly dissipated when I got close enough to see what someone had done.

I had tried to make my room feel cozy by hanging a curtain of beads around my desk and tacking up postcards of the places I wanted to visit. Someone had ripped my postcards off of the walls and torn them into tiny pieces like hamster bedding. My dresser had been emptied and my clothing slashed with scissors, then thrown everywhere. On the wall behind the bed, "Go Home Hippie" had been written in ruby lipstick over and over again, in seven sloppy rows that wrapped around the corner of the wall, stopping just shy of the window sill. The strands of beads had been pulled apart one by one and scattered. As I tried to examine the damage, I slipped on them and crashed onto the floor.

"Damn it!" I rubbed my left ankle which had twisted beneath me when I fell.

I screamed so loudly that I was surprised the window didn't break. I couldn't contain myself, nor did I try. I was injured and scared and tired of being treated like shit by people who didn't know me. I unleashed another horrific scream which quickly turned into a chorus of ugly sobs and heaving. Never had I felt so pathetic in all my life, and so alien. Why was I even bothering with school anyway? Clearly I didn't belong there after all.

"Holy shit," someone said behind me. Pat must've heard me and come running to the scene. I hadn't even noticed him climb in through the window.

"Y-you aren't supposed to be here," I stuttered as he knelt down, scooping me into his arms.

He pulled me in close and rested his chin softly on my head. "Don't worry about that. Actually, don't worry about any of this." He reached into his pocket and retrieved a pack of cigarettes. He placed the box in my palms and I curled my fingers around it. "Go outside and enjoy these. Let Mother Nature take care of you while I clean this up, ok?"

I nodded and he helped me into a standing position. My ankle ached when I put pressure on it, but not enough to dissuade me from getting the hell out of there.

"You sure you don't want to smoke one with me?" I asked. So much for cutting the habit.

"Nah, you go ahead. I don't like to smoke unless I'm real stressed."

I limped my way outside trying my best not to break down again. I sat on the nearest bench and smoked one cigarette after another until my humiliation turned into anger. Once I had burned through several of them, I threw the pack onto the pavement and marched straight to room 103 of Parker Hall.

Professor Hodge was in the middle of lecturing a group of upperclassmen, but I didn't care. I banged my fists against the door, imagining the hinges flying off like bullet casings. He waved me away, so I began shaking the doorknob with the force of a blender on high speed.

"I'll be right back," he said unable to ignore me any longer. He came out into the hallway, closing the door behind him. "What the hell is the matter with you?" he spat.

I swallowed a lump that had lodged itself in my throat. I tried to respond, but words failed me.

Concern spread across his features. "You look like you've been cheated by the devil, and you smell like a chimney sweep." A colleague passed by and all signs of sympathy disappeared. "Now out with it. I don't take kindly to being interrupted so abruptly. I have a class to teach you know."

I took a deep breath and explained everything that had happened. Students passing by paled and quickened their pace, terrified by my exaggerated arm movements and tomato face. I can't say that I blamed them. If I looked as crazed as I felt, they had every right to run.

Once I was finished he glanced down at his watch. "Is that all, Ms. Carter?"

I wanted to slap him. "Excuse me?"

"I asked if that was all. I have to get back to my students. We only have fifteen minutes remaining, and a whole chapter to cover. You understand how things are." He placed his hand on the knob of his door and twisted it. It was looser than ever, as a result of my assault on it. His students peered out at me curiously through the crack. Some of them sniggered.

"No, actually I don't understand," I said.

He shifted his weight from one foot to the other. "Look, I'm sorry this happened to you, but there's nothing I can do. If you have been emotionally disturbed by this incident, I recommend you see a guidance counselor."

"That's *it*?" I asked, crossing my arms. "Is there someone else I should report it to? Someone who can bring justice? You did hear what I said, didn't you? They wrecked my stuff!"

Professor Hodge shook his head. "Ordinarily I would recommend reporting this incident to one of the deans. But being that you and Pat insist on being so...well...*different* from the rest of your peers, I'm not sure that you should bother bringing it to their attention. They'll likely chastise you for wasting their time and tell you to dress more appropriately. You are aware of the dress code are you not?"

I didn't know what irritated me more. His lack of a solution, or his bringing up my outfit. I didn't see how what I wore had anything to do with the situation.

"*Wasting* their time?" my voice quivered. "So people can just ruin my belongings and piss me off whenever they want to and nobody is going to do anything about it? You're saying that nobody cares?"

Hodge swung open the door. Several kids whispered "Shhh be quiet. He's back!" Hodge gave them a warning look, and then turned to me a final time. "Precisely. That's just the way things are Ms. Carter. I recommend you lock the door to your room, and do your best to blend in from now on. It's easier that way for *all* of us."

After dealing with Hodge, the last thing I felt like doing was returning to my room. I wasn't ready to confront the disaster that awaited me there, even though Pat had promised to take care of it. I felt sort of bad leaving him alone to clean, but I wasn't strong enough to see it the way it was when I had left. I knew I would've just crumpled into another heap of ugly sobs, and been sent out with another cigarette.

I paced around campus, glaring at everyone I passed. I didn't know who among them was guilty of destroying my things, but in some ways I decided that they all were. Who among them had defended me as people spat on my food in the cafeteria, or tripped me on my way to class? Who among them hadn't accused me of being dirty or on drugs or some other stupid stereotype?

When I returned to my room a few hours later, all evidence of what had occurred was gone. There was no lipstick on the walls or beads on the floor. A groovy mauve tapestry had been hung where the postcards used to be. Pat's turntable sat on the desk, with the needle carefully positioned so that when I turned it on it played "I Got You Babe." Beside it was a note with sloppy handwriting that said: "Got kicked out by your roommate. Take your time with my turntable and relax. Don't worry about the tapestry. It looks better in your place anyway. When you're ready I'll be waiting in the library. We can buy you more clothes tonight."

I smiled and clutched the note to my chest. I swayed back and forth to the music and soon enough my mood flipped. I giggled to myself thinking about how erratic the day had been, and how swiftly my mood had changed from one extreme to the next.

Maybe I was as weird as everyone thought. And maybe I *was* a little crazy after all. But I'd be damned if I quit school because of the clones. I couldn't let them get the best of me; I couldn't let those assholes win.

Chapter 5: October 31st, 1968

Clink.

Clink.

I woke up from a nap and peered around the room. One of my history books slid off of my stomach and onto the floor, along with a blank piece of paper. I hadn't gotten very far with my homework before nodding off. It turned out I wasn't all that interested in Charlemagne and his conquests.

Clink.

I yawned and pinpointed that the sound was coming from the window.

Clink.

It was Pat chucking little grey stones at it, like Romeo in bell bottoms. Seeing me, he picked up a small boulder and pretended like he was going to throw that too. I slid the window open, frowning at a bug that had died between the glass.

"Jeez Pat. Give me a chance to get up," I said more harshly than I had intended.

"Yikes; someone's cranky. Am I interrupting something?"

"Sort of," I said, back-pedaling my 'tude. "What do you want?"

"It's *Halloween*."

I glanced at my calendar and realized he was right. That explained the paper skeletons that were strung up in the common room and why my art professor had passed around a bowl of candy corn earlier.

"So?" I asked.

"What do you mean 'so'? Don't you celebrate?"

I sighed, kind of wishing he'd go away already. My back was beginning to hurt from leaning out of the window. "Not so much anymore," I said.

"Well that's boring. Why don't you come out of there and we'll celebrate it together."

I shook my head, recalling all of the work I had left to do. "No thanks, I think I'll stay in. I have a lot of homework."

He placed his hands on his hips like my mother did when she was disappointed in me. "You can copy mine if it means you'll hang out with me."

"You're done already? How's that possible?"

He grinned sideways, shrugging as though it were nothing. "I'm fast, that's all. So are you coming or not?"

I considered his offer. I wasn't a fan of cheating, but it was certainly tempting. If I didn't copy his homework, I wasn't sure whether I'd be able to finish it on my own, on account of my tendency to doze off. Would it really hurt if I bent the rules?

"Fine. I'll be right out," I said.

Standing at the window had reminded me how chilly it was outside. I changed into a thicker top and put on my suede jacket. I crawled through my window and clumsily hopped down.

"So what's the plan, Stan?" I asked. "We're not trick-or-treating I hope."

Pat laughed and said sarcastically, "Nah I gave that up last year. What do you want to do?"

I contemplated this. What *did* I want to do? When I was a kid my mom walked me around town to show off whatever costume she had made me that year. The neighbors all gawked at her talent, secretly disappointed that their children's outfits paled in comparison. One year I was a jack-o'-lantern with a green curly headpiece and sequined tights. Another I was a witch with a broom made out of shiny gold pipe cleaners. The concepts were never the most creative; my mom didn't want me looking outlandish. But the execution was something to be admired.

Once I hit middle school it felt weird being paraded around by my mom, so I called it a quits. She assigned me candy duty which I eagerly took on, but it wasn't the same. The magic of the season was gone. My parents took note of this lack of enthusiasm and stopped putting out decorations and purchasing pumpkins. By high school we didn't even hand out candy.

"I want to carve a pumpkin," I said at last. "And eat candy until my teeth rot out." I bared my teeth to show him I meant business.

"I like it," he said. "I know a patch about a mile from here."

"Murphy's?" I asked.

"That's the one. I always forget you grew up around here. It's a shame you were forced to go to private school; even my parents weren't *that* stuck-up. Public school is where it's at."

"Yeah I bet."

Silence fell over us so he continued, "I figure we can go to Murphy's as long as it's not too busy. Then we can cut through town and get our candy on the way back."

"Cool. What about a knife to carve with? Do you have one?"

He flipped open his pocket-knife which had a brass handle and clean blade. "This should do alright, as long as we get ones with thin skin."

I stepped back and inspected the knife at a distance. I didn't know why this object unnerved me. It wasn't like I had never seen one before. My dad used his every autumn to peel the apples that fell from our neighbor's tree and into our backyard. My grandfather had used his on fishing trips.

"Actually, I have a better idea," I said thinking on my feet. "Let's paint the pumpkins."

Pat put the knife away and I exhaled.

"Whatever floats your boat. That's probably easier anyway," he said. "Do you happen to have paint, or do we need to buy that too? I don't have a lot of cash on me."

"Yep I've got paint. And plenty of it," I responded, already imagining various ways of decorating my pumpkin. Although my parents weren't happy that I was taking an art course this semester, they had still made sure I had an ample amount of everything I could possibly need: paper, paint, brushes, charcoal, and clay. You name it I had it, and all of professional quality. My parents would've been pissed if they knew some of it was about to be "wasted" on a gourd.

"Great," Pat said. "Let's get going."

The pumpkin patch was congested with clones, all hay riding with their dates and eating fresh apple-cider donuts. The air smelled like straw and mud with a hint of frying oil. Pat and I boarded the first available wagon, which took us out to the field where we could pick our own pumpkins.

The actual field wasn't crowded. We guessed that most of the clones didn't want to risk getting their shift dresses dirty. The ground was muddy on account of the rain that had drenched it the night before. We walked slowly to avoid slipping, but that didn't stop Pat from taking a spill. When he stood up it looked like he had pooped his pants. He couldn't stop laughing at himself, joking that he should lay off the Brussel sprouts. I told him that he was an embarrassment to society and he shoved me playfully, but not hard enough to make me fall.

We ambled around until I stumbled upon a pumpkin that was rounder than a globe and bright orange. "This is the one," I exclaimed, wrapping my arms around it. It slid out of my hands as I tried to pick it up, and rolled along the slick ground.

"No it's not," Pat said bluntly.

"Yes it is," I said chasing after it.

He waited patiently for me to catch up to it, and then watched as I struggled to lift it. My back cracked as I pressed the pumpkin against my chest and attempted to straighten up.

"Are you really going to lug that thing a mile back?" he asked.

I nodded, determined not to give up on my perfect pumpkin, even as my grip began to fail.

"Ok then. But are you also going to lug it through the store when we get our candy? Then back to the school?"

Unable to hold it any longer, it plopped onto the ground, narrowly avoiding my feet. It split open from the impact, having been dropped one too many times.

"I could've put it in a cart," I argued.

"Of course you could've," Pat said. The corners of his mouth turned upward, but he didn't make fun of me. Instead he pointed to two smaller pumpkins whose flesh were speckled green and vines intertwined. "How about these? They're sort of cool. It's like they're morphing into watermelons."

I easily lifted the larger of the two up. "Oh yeah, these are much better. Well spotted."

"Thanks."

We road back to the main part of the patch and purchased our pumpkins. On our way out several clones jeered at us for being dirty hippies, and for once they were right. We really were filthy. But we had a hell of a lot more fun than any of them.

After getting our candy and changing into clean clothes, we brought our pumpkins to room 103 of Parker Hall. We scattered newspaper along the floor to avoid making too much of a mess, and placed a pyramid of chocolate bars between us. Pat held his pumpkin on his lap as he worked, not caring that more paint was getting on his outfit than on the gourd. I lay on my stomach so that my pumpkin was at eye level, working carefully. Unlike him, I wouldn't have bothered getting changed if I intended on getting paint all over myself.

Pat finished much sooner than I did, and ate one candy bar after the next until most of our stash was gone. It was a wonder he was as skinny as he was, given the amount of food he consumed on a regular basis. I had once watched him eat three veggie burgers in one sitting, then wash them down with a banana smoothie. Not an hour later, he insisted we stop for ice cream sundaes from our favorite shop. Either he had multiple stomachs, or the one that he had was endless.

After eating his weight in chocolate, he went out into the hallway to take a drink from the water fountain. When he came back he tapped his fingers against the desktops, singing songs of his own invention with a look of pure joy on his face. I did my best not to get distracted by him, wanting to finish before midnight.

"That should do it," I said after a while. "I'll show you mine if you show me yours."

His face flushed as he grabbed his pumpkin and turned it towards me. It was the goofiest looking thing that I had ever seen. He had painted it light blue and used a black marker to add three googly eyes and buck teeth. There were two squiggly marks on each side of its face which I assumed were supposed to be ears, and several swatches of pink that didn't make any sense. After thoroughly inspecting his kindergartener's project, I tried my best to appear impressed. In reality I was glad that I had found something he wasn't good at. I was beginning to think he was a robot or something.

"His name is Harold," he said seriously. "He loves American cheese and is allergic to pineapple. His greatest aspiration is to find a Mrs. Harold. He's afraid of camels, but only if they're not wearing hats."

"Wow you've really thought this through," I said, giggling. "He's a very cute little monster."

"Thanks, I had plenty of time to think of a backstory. You took forever. But what makes you say he's a monster?"

I drew my eyebrows together. I really had no good answer to this. It was an innocent question, but philosophical all the same. What defines a monster?

He interrupted my thoughts. "Aren't you going to show me what you've been working so hard on?"

"Oh, right."

He put Harold down and I handed my pumpkin to him. I had used pastel variations of every color in the rainbow to create a tie-dyed effect, then splatter painted it with white. It wasn't a very festive pumpkin, unless we were celebrating Easter, but it was eye-catching. I had even taken the time to paint the stem elephant grey.

He whistled, observing it at every angle. "Yep. I'm afraid it's just as I thought."

"What?" I asked, taking it back from him. It hadn't fully dried so some of the paint came off on his fingers, leaving parts of the pumpkin bare. I returned it to the floor to touch it up.

"You should be an art major," he said. "If you can take a weird-ass pumpkin and make it beautiful, I can only imagine what you can do on a proper canvas. You'll have to show me your other work some time."

I ignored him focused solely on fixing my project.

"June?" he asked.

"Hmm?"

"Are you even listening?"

I blew on my pumpkin so that the paint would dry a little faster, and then set my brush down. "Yeah, you think I should be an artist."

"Only if you want to of course."

I wiped my hands on the newsprint. It made them feel even dirtier, and I couldn't wait to give them a good scrub. "Is that really an option?" I asked.

He took my hands into his own and looked me straight in the eyes. They were bluer than ever, and easy to trust.

"Everything is an option," he said softly.

He released my filthy hands, and I studied a speck of paint that had dripped onto the floor. Seeing what I was looking at, Pat scraped it off with his thumb.

"If you say so," I said.

I gathered our paintbrushes into a pile. Newspaper clung to the bristles, so I took my time plucking it off until they were clean.

Pat seemed to recognize that I was contemplating something, and remained silent as he threw away his candy wrappers followed by the towels that we had used to clean our brushes between colors. He tipped over our Dixie cups which had been filled with murky brown water, and got another batch of towels to wipe it up with.

Everything is an option, I thought over and over again. *Everything* is an option.

Chapter 6: November 23rd, 1968

"Happy birthday!" Pat exclaimed as I walked into room 103. It was decorated with branches, leaves, and rocks that he had collected outside and arranged around the room. I couldn't decide whether it looked more like an enchanted forest or a hobo camp, but I appreciated the effort. I put my blanket and Christmas lights on a desk and gave him a quick hug.

"It looks great in here," I said, not sure if this was entirely truthful. "You know you really didn't have to do all this. Nineteen isn't exactly a special age."

Pat looked genuinely hurt. "Not special? Every age is special, June. It means you've survived another year on this crazy planet. Death doesn't discriminate you know." He handed me a lumpy package that had been wrapped with the comics section of the newspaper and so much masking tape that it appeared mummified.

"What's this?" I asked, struggling to tear it open.

Pat took out his pocket knife and cut open one end so that I could slide the gift out of the paper.

Inside was a white t-shirt with yellow daisies framing the phrase "Itty Bitty Titty Committee." I snorted as I read it. Any other girl would've been offended by receiving this from a guy, but I was amused. Pat and I had no qualms about poking fun at each other's skinny-ass bodies. We both knew we were bony, no bones about it.

"If only I had been wearing this earlier," I laughed, removing my blouse and putting the t-shirt on instead. It was softer than I had expected and smelled like earth and cologne.

Pat politely looked away as I changed, only peeking once to see if I was done. "What? Was some jerk staring at your foam domes again?"

I spread my blanket across the floor and sat on it. "Not exactly," I hesitated, not knowing how to proceed. "It's just that on my way over here I was stopped by that kid, Jesse Mann. You know, the one in Anders' class. I think he's a year ahead of us. Maybe two."

"Is that the dude on the basketball team? The one whose head practically skims the ceiling?"

"Yeah, that's him." I avoided Pat's eyes, creeped out by the fact that he had barely blinked since the beginning of this conversation. "Anyway, he invited me to his party tonight. He said that all of his friends will be there and that he'd like to introduce me to them. He insisted that it'll be a good time and that he wants to get to know me." I hesitated to tell him the rest. "He also said that he thinks I'm cute."

Now it was Pat's turn to avoid my gaze. He put his hands in his pockets and slumped forward. "What did you tell him?"

"I told him that I'd think about it. I mean, I really don't know the guy but I guess he could be cool. Maybe he's different from the rest of the clones. If I had been wearing this shirt I would've known his true intentions." I had meant the last part as a joke, but Pat didn't laugh.

Instead he nodded and took out a cigarette. He held it stiffly but didn't light it right away. He seemed to be thinking about something. "If you go to the party I'm coming with you," he said at last.

"No you aren't," I said curtly. "You'll be miserable the whole night. You hate parties and crowds."

"So do you," he said.

He had a point there.

"Has this kid ever talked to you before? Or shown any sign of interest at all?" he asked.

Heat radiated throughout my body and I clutched my knees towards my chest. "Not really. But he hasn't acted revolted by my presence like everyone else. Doesn't that count for something?"

Pat twirled the cigarette between his fingers and joined me on the floor. He put on a Bob Dylan album that we had stolen from the radio station, and listened to the first couple of songs without comment. I assumed that the conversation had been dropped, so I allowed my mind to wander.

Should I dress casually for the party, or put some effort into my appearance? Would there be food? I hoped so. I wasn't a pretty eater, but I could sneak snacks when nobody was watching. What did normal people eat at college parties anyway? Pretzels? Chips? Was I supposed to bring a bag of them with me or would they be there when I arrived?

"I'm still coming," Pat said breaking the silence. "I just don't trust it, June. You barely know the guy. I won't hang around you all night if that's what you're worried about. I just want to keep an eye out."

"Suit yourself," I said bitterly. I was offended that he thought I couldn't take care of myself. Who was he to judge how I spent my time and who I spent it with? My mind swirled with dozens of questions, none of which I had answers for.

Truthfully, I *had* thought it was weird that Jesse asked me to the party. And I wasn't sure that I wanted to go. Something about the whole thing seemed wrong, but I couldn't pinpoint the reason for my hesitation. The only way to figure it out was to go to the damn thing and see how it went. The experience would be worth it even if all I learned was the ins and outs of what normal people do on a Saturday night, and why our dorm bathrooms were always disgusting the next day.

At half past nine we headed over to the apartment building on the edge of campus. The building was imposing, made of weathered brick that contrasted against fat ivory pillars and black window railings. It had been a hospital from the inception of the town all the way up through the Second World War. Once the war was over they converted it into an apartment complex so that they could open up a new hospital somewhere better situated. At least, that's what the brochure from orientation said. I had heard rumors that it was so haunted that they ran out of staff members who were willing to take the night shift. Now the apartments were mainly populated with college kids who were either too dumb to notice the paranormal activity or too drunk to care. That and ghosts hiding textbooks are more easily ignored than ghosts hiding a patient's oxygen tank.

We walked up the steps and, like the party newbs we were, knocked on the front door. When nobody answered we opened it and were greeted by the sharp stench of sweat and vodka. The hallway ahead of us was packed with girls and boys clutching half empty cups of some green alcoholic concoction. Music reverberated off the walls, giving me an immediate headache. I rubbed my throbbing temples as we waded through the crowd in search of Jesse.

"Excuse me," I said tapping on some girl's shoulder. Judging by her uniform she was a cheerleader. Judging by the puddle of liquid that was dribbled down the front of her shirt, she was drunk. "Do you know where Jesse Mann is?"

She burped. "Ummmm…" Her inebriated mind struggled to formulate a logical response. It was painful to watch. I imagined the inside of her brain looking like a bunch of glittery cogs all gunked up with grey chewing gum.

"I think he's in there," she said, pointing at a room several feet away. "Well, that's where he lives at least."

"Thanks." It was the only lead we had, so we went with it.

Pat grabbed my hand and we pushed our way through the crowd until we made it safely into the apartment where she said Jesse would be. The room was dark except for a few blinking lights, making it nearly impossible to see. We stood in the threshold, allowing our eyes to adjust to the poor lighting.

Eventually I could make out that there were four figures huddled around some sort of a makeshift bar. One of them was moving towards us.

"Well look who made it," the figure said. I recognized the voice as Jesse's. It had a distinctive rusty quality, like it had been left out in the sun to dry. "I see you brought a friend. I have to admit, I'd hoped it would be just us."

He drew closer holding two bottles of booze. He handed one to me and the other to Pat. I attempted a smile but doubted it looked sincere. Something about his towering figure and slurred speech made me nervous. I instantly hated him.

"Do you think you could give us some space?" Jesse asked, scowling at Pat. "Don't you have some sort of an orgie to attend or something?"

Pat's hand tensed in mine. I hadn't realized he was still holding it.

"Classy," Pat mumbled under his breath.

"What did you say?" Jesse spat, stepping towards Pat.

Pat took a step back. "Nothing. Nothing at all."

"That's what I thought." Jesse gazed down at our hands which were still interlocked. "Oh, don't tell me you two are some sort of an item," he asked.

I released Pat's hand. "No, we're just friends," I said casually.

"Good." Jesse reached forward and stroked my cheek with his sticky fingers. I backed away from him, but he advanced.

Pat looked like he was going to kill him.

"What's the matter with your drink?" Jesse asked, nodding at me.

"Huh?"

"Your drink. You haven't touched it. I can get you something else if you want. How about some Fireball? Or are you one of those cocktail snobs?"

"Actually," I said, "I think I need some air."

"But you just got here," Jesse whined. His speech was getting progressively worse. "Sit down. Relax. We're all friends here. You, me, even this clown you brought with you."

"No thanks," I said glancing sideways. "Are you coming with?" I asked Pat.

He shook his head and took a swig of his drink. "I think I'd like to talk to Jesse for a bit. See what he's all about."

"Are you sure?" I asked. Leaning in closely I added, "Something doesn't feel right. I don't trust him as far as I can throw him."

"I'll be out of here before you know it," he said. "Okay?"

"If you say so," I handed him my bottle. "Just don't cause any trouble," I whispered.

Pat took another drink, this time from the bottle that had been mine. I took this as my cue to leave. My headache had only become worse since entering the room, and I was eager to get away from the intoxicated environment that most college kids found enjoyable.

Once outside, I thought about going back and telling Pat that Jesse wasn't worth it. There was no need to figure out "what he was all about." If I had been a better friend I never would have left him behind. What good could have come from him staying there alone? Instead I sat on a bench counting stars until I became too drowsy to sit upright. I laid down on the smooth wooden surface and drifted off to sleep, only waking when the complex's front door slammed shut several hours later.

I opened my eyes expecting to see a drunk frat brother passed out on the lawn. Instead Pat was hovering over me. His lip was cut open, but the blood was already dry. His arms were covered with colossal bruises, and his shirt was poking through the fly of his unzipped pants. His eyes were black and lifeless, their sky blue brilliance tainted by terror.

"What the hell happened in there?" I asked, rolling to a standing position. I took his head into my hands. His skin was clammy, and he winced as I traced a scratch along his jawline. "You look like shit. Did Jesse and his band of assholes beat you up?"

Pat refused to look at me and vomited on the grass. I stood behind him and held his hair out of the way. He continued to hurl until his stomach was empty and the vomiting turned to dry heaving. When he was through I lifted him up and wrapped my arms around him for support.

"Come on," I said, as though he was actually listening, "let's get you back to your dorm. We can talk about this tomorrow."

We walked back in silence, the moon our only source of light. I wondered what time it was, given that the streetlamps had been turned off.

When we finally arrived at his building, Pat went in without saying "Goodnight," "Thank you," or even "See you later." I doubted he realized I was there.

Chapter 7: November 24th, 1968

The morning after the party, I got dressed and rushed over to the student lounge. It was only 8:00am, but I was eager to speak to Pat. I hadn't slept for more than five minutes the previous night, too busy thinking about what may have happened at the party. I hoped that at least Pat had gotten some shuteye. He had looked so tired when I left him, and so fragile. Like a G.I returning from his first battle.

When I got to the lounge I pulled the directory off of the shelf above the phones. I quickly skimmed through the list of buildings until I found the number for the boys' dormitory.

A clone yawned into the receiver. "Gregory Hall, Head Resident speaking. How may I help you?"

"Uh. Hi," I began. "This is June Carter. I was wondering if I could talk to Pat."

"Pat? Pat who?"

"Pat...uh...well I don't actually know his last name," I admitted. I had never thought to ask what it was, and he never wrote his full name on assignments. He was always just "Pat" to me and everyone else who knew him. Even the professors didn't address him formally.

"What does he look like?" the Head Resident asked.

"He has shoulder length hair and blue eyes. Oh, and he wears a lot of jeans."

"Shoulder length hair, huh? Is he sort of a hippie?"

"Yes that's the one."

I could practically hear the Head Resident roll his eyes. "I'll go knock on his door. Hang on a moment."

After a long pause, the clone came back on the line. "Are you still there?" he asked.

"Yeah, I'm here."

"Listen, I banged on the door, but he wouldn't answer it. Maybe he's still sleeping. It is the weekend you know."

"Maybe," I said doubtfully. Pat once told me that he liked to rise with the sun. He said it was the natural way of things, and that he liked to be in tune with nature. The sun had come up a half hour ago, when I was lying in bed staring up at a crack in the ceiling. If Pat wasn't up, something had to be wrong.

"What about his roommate?" I asked. "Isn't his roommate around to answer the door?"

"Let me see," he shuffled some papers. "No, it appears that he went home for the weekend."

"Are you sure?"

"Yes ma'am. It's written right here in the log."

"Well that sucks."

The Head Resident yawned again. "If there's nothing else I can do for you, I really should get going..."

I interrupted him. "What room is Pat in?"

"Why do you need to know?"

"I'd like to send him a care package that's all," I lied. "I'm his sister."

"A sister that doesn't know his last name?"

Shit.

"What I meant to say is that I'm *like* his sister. We grew up together, but lost touch. I rang his folks and they said that I'd find him here, but they said he had changed his last name as a way of cutting ties with them. They weren't sure what he had changed it to."

Fuck I was bad at lying. Only a real dipstick would buy that story.

The clone sounded suspicious, but gave in. "He's in room 306, but you can just address the package to Gregory Hall. I'll make sure that it gets to him, no problem."

"Thank you." I hung up the phone then jogged to the boys' dormitory. I had to find out if Pat was ok, no matter the cost. He would've done the same for me. I peered through the double doors at the entrance just as a group of clones was about to come out. They strode past me, wearing fancy jackets and ties for church. One of them elbowed me out of their way.

"Watch it, longhair," he threatened. "Don't you have anything better to do than to spy on us? Or are you just high?"

"Shut the hell up," I shouted, surprised by my boldness.

"What did you say to me?" he stopped in his tracks.

I clenched my fists. I was fed up with the way Pat and I had been treated the last few months, and my fatigue was making me feisty. "I said S-H-U-T the hell up. That's shut the hell up. Get the picture? I wouldn't spy on you if you were the last men alive."

He raised his arm like he was going to punch me, but his friend held him back.

"Aw leave her alone, John," his friend said. "We're going to be late, and you shouldn't hit a girl."

"I'm not sure she qualifies as one," John said. He spat on my shoe and added, "But I'll give her this one pass."

I waited for them to leave before flipping them off. I wiped my shoe in the grass, disgusted by the wet oval that his saliva had left behind. I quickly put my shoe back on, and peered once more through the glass. Seeing no one but the Head Resident, I entered.

The Head Resident was too busy filling out a pink slip to pay me any attention, mumbling something about missing ping pong paddles and drunks. I easily tiptoed around him before climbing the stairs. It didn't take me long to reach the third floor, and room 306. I knocked twice.

"Pat, it's me." I whispered through the crack.

No answer. Not event a grunt.

"Pat, if you're in there let me in." Raising my voice I added, "I'll get in a shitload of trouble if someone finds me here. Hell, some guy almost beat me up just five minutes ago when I was trying to find a way in. I'm not leaving until you talk to me."

A minute went by then the door swung open. Pat stood before me, wearing the same clothes as the night before. Traces of dried blood still clung to his lips, and his breath reeked of vomit. I covered my mouth to avoid gagging.

"Oh God. Let's get you cleaned up," I said ushering him into his room. It was messier than I had imagined it, with soda bottles and empty cans of deodorant everywhere. I pulled a fresh set of clothing out of his dresser, and set it on his bed. I pinched the bottom of his shirt and attempted to help him off with it, but he recoiled so I stopped.

"Sorry," I said. "Did that hurt?"

No response.

"Alright then...why don't you get dressed while I get something to wash your face with?" This time I knew better than to expect an answer. I grabbed a wad of tissues then went out into the hallway to soak them with water from the fountain. I did this slowly, wanting to leave him with enough time to get changed. When I got back, Pat was exactly as I had left him.

"Here," I said, gently bathing his face and neck. He allowed me to help him, but stared blankly at the wall behind me. Blood seeped into the tissues turning them pink. I threw them into the trash bin, already overflowing with balls of paper and candy wrappers.

"How about we get some breakfast?" I asked.

He shook his head.

"You need to eat. We don't have to go to the dining hall if you don't want. I'll buy you something out. Then maybe you can tell me what happened."

"No." He said firmly.

"No to breakfast or no to talking?" I asked.

"No."

I threw my hands up at him. It was one thing not to get dressed, but another not to speak full sentences to me. "If you don't tell me what happened last night, I'll just ask Jesse tomorrow after class. Is that what you want?"

A vein in his neck pulsed, and he began clawing at his forearm. Red scratches appeared where his fingernails dug into his skin. One of them started to bleed, and he focused his efforts on furthering this wound. I reached over to stop him from hurting himself more than he already had, but he shook me off.

"Don't you dare talk to him," he said.

"Then tell me what happened," I snapped.

He bowed his head into his hands and began to sob.

I instantly regretted being so forceful. It was the first time I had ever seen a man cry, and I hoped to never see it again. It was heartbreaking and raw—the most real thing that I had ever witnessed. Pat was hurting and I had hurt him, making me feel guilty beyond words. But what I didn't understand was what had made him so vulnerable to begin with. What had caused Pat to become so moody? I had never known him to be anything but content until now.

"Alright," I said. "I promise that I won't talk to Jesse, and I won't force you to eat. Not today at least."

Pat lifted his head, and I thought he was going to say something. Instead he climbed into bed and pulled the covers around him. I waited for him to fall asleep, and then watched as his

chest rose up and down slowly, evenly. After a while I left, not

knowing what more I could do to help him.

Chapter 8: December 13th, 1968

Old man winter came late to the party, and Jack Frost must've had better things to do. It was almost Christmas but we hadn't had more than a flurry of snow, and I hadn't been able to wear my new patchwork coat. Even though I wasn't much of a winter girl, I had been hoping for a snowstorm by now. I wanted to see the campus all decked out with snow and icicles, and to go sledding down the hill by the gym on cafeteria trays.

So far winter had been dreary and grey: the opposite of a wonderland. I found myself humming "California Dreaming" more than usual, much to the dismay of my roommate whose musical taste was confined to Elvis, Elvis, and more Elvis. Anytime I tried to play my own music, she'd turn on one of his albums at full blast.

It turned into a bit of a competition between her and me. Who could play their music the loudest without getting yelled at by the Head Resident? We spent so much time blasting music at one another that eventually the needle on her turntable snapped off. I was happy when this happened, but wasn't a jerk about it. I told her that when I wasn't around, she could borrow my turntable until she got a replacement needle.

Pat and I hadn't spent nearly as much time together since the night of the party. Lately he looked lost, like a ghost that didn't realize they were dead yet. We mainly stuck to our routine of chilling in Parker Hall on Saturdays, decking it out with Christmas lights and other groovy things. Unlike before, he didn't hang around for long. He looked distracted for what little time he was with me then pretended to have something to take care of and left. He never even helped clean up anymore; he just left me alone to deal with it all. I assumed he was still mad at me for snapping at him the month prior, but on the off chance that he wasn't, I didn't want to remind him of what an asshole I'd been.

The night before my parents were due to pick me up for break, I was sitting on my bed painting my fingernails violet while listening to the college's radio station. I wasn't about to paint them red or pink or any of the other colors that my mom recommended, but violet wasn't too bad. At least this way my mom wouldn't chastise me for how dirty they were.

The song, "I'm so Tired" blared through the radio's speakers and I waited for the lyrics to begin skipping. I had stolen *The White Album* two weeks prior, shocked that the station had bought something so new. I was eating carrots while listening to it, and spilled a bottle of ranch dressing all over it. In my attempt to clean the record, I scratched it to death and smeared grease in all of the grooves.

About twenty seconds in, the lyrics became garbled until they were completely unintelligible. The radio hosts turned it off, apologizing for the poor quality. One of them commented on how weird the album smelled: like socks that had been stuffed with garlic. I guessed that this was a result of my accident too. They put on the damn Faith Tones for the third time that evening so I switched the station.

When the door creaked open I didn't bother looking up. I had forgotten that my roommate had already gone home for break, and assumed that she was just coming back from her job at the library. Without Pat to hang out with, I had grown used to seeing her come in and asking her about her day. Her tales never proved very interesting, but I pretended to listen anyway.

"Hey," a male voice said.

I knocked over my nail polish and it spilled on my quilt.

Pat stepped fully into the room and closed the door behind him. "Shit, sorry about that." He grabbed a fistful of tissues from my side table and began blotting at the mess. I inspected his work, and stopped him. He was only making it worse.

"What are you doing here?" I asked. "And how come you didn't use the window?"

He reeked of tobacco, but looked pretty good.

"I didn't feel like climbing, so I picked the lock on the back door. I wanted to see you before you left." He smiled and tucked his hair behind his ears.

God how I missed that smile.

"You're lucky that you didn't run into anyone," I said.

"I would've talked my way out of it," he shrugged. "Do you want to take a walk or something?"

"Hell yes," I said. I hopped down from my bed nearly tipping my mattress out of its frame. I'd have said yes to anything short of going to another party.

He handed me the jacket that I had laid out to wear the next day, and I slid it on over my camisole.

"Oh—before I forget," I said, peering around the room. I found what I was looking for on the windowsill and handed it to Pat. It was the Rolling Stones album that had been released a few days earlier. I hadn't had the chance to wrap it. "Merry Christmas."

He traced the cover with his thumb and the grin that he had flashed earlier returned tenfold. "This is too much," he said looking over the track list. "Thank you."

"You're welcome."

He held the album with one hand and put the other in his pocket, feeling for something. "Ready to head out?" He asked.

"Yep. Ready when you are."

We trudged uphill, away from the dormitories and towards the heart of campus. Pat didn't say anything, and neither did I. We were beyond the stage of having to fill the silence with useless small talk. When the wind kicked up, making my hands look translucent, Pat handed me his fingerless gloves. They were moist on the inside as though he had been sweating, so I didn't feel bad about borrowing them.

He took out a cigarette and placed it between his teeth. He struggled to light it on account of the weather, but eventually managed to. I coughed when the smoke blew in my direction. I hadn't smoked in over a month so my lungs had begun to heal; they weren't thrilled about breathing toxic air secondhand. Taking notice, Pat switched places with me.

We arrived at the library and he tossed the cancer stick to the ground, only to replace it with another. We stood there for several minutes as he finished his second one, and I asked him if he'd mind if I went inside to get warm.

"Wait," he said, biting his lower lip. He looked down at the cigarettes he had smeared against the cement.

I worried that he was retreating into a bad place again; the one that made him leave me on short notice.

"I was going to give you your gift after you got back, but I guess now is as good a time as any." He fumbled in his pocket and retrieved a small box with a green bow.

I wasted no time in opening the present. Even though he had gotten me something for my birthday, I hadn't expected anything for Christmas. Inside of the box was a sleek silver chain with a pink crystal pendant. He helped me put it on and it sat comfortably between my collar bones. I held it between two fingers and stroked it; it was smooth and slightly cool to the touch.

"It's a Rose Quartz," he said. "The lady who sold it to me said they attract love and peace and all sorts of other good vibes. She also said that they dispel negativity." He shifted from one foot to the other. I could tell that he was debating something, but what?

"This is really, *really* nice," I said. "Now I feel sort of bad that I only got you that album."

"Are you kidding? That's the best gift you could have gotten me. I love getting albums from people. It takes a lot of thought to buy someone the right one."

"I'm glad you liked it," I said. "I wasn't sure if you were a Stones guy or not."

"I can be," he said. "When the mood strikes."

"That's good I guess."

We stared at each other silently. After several minutes had passed, I moved towards the door, hinting that I still wanted to go inside.

"Hey June?" he asked.

"Yeah, Pat?"

"What do you think about being more than friends? You know, like girlfriend and boyfriend?"

I hesitated, and his face fell. Truthfully, I had never thought it was a possibility. He didn't seem like the type of guy to date girls, even though he was more handsome than Jesus Christ. I never thought he was gay or anything; I'd seen him check out girls from time to time. I just thought he was too much of a free spirit to seriously commit to someone.

I knew that he made me happy and that I admired him more than anyone. And I knew that I felt warm around him, and comforted by his touch. But was a relationship the right way to go? Or would it just ruin our friendship?

"Oh Pat, I don't know." I said. "You've been kind of weird lately. Every time we hang out it's like you just want to leave. I thought you were mad at me and too chicken shit to tell me that you don't want to be friends anymore."

He frowned. "I know, and I'm sorry for that. I just needed to work through some things on my own. That's all. I don't blame you if you don't want to go out with me after the way I've been acting. But I'd really like it if you'd give me the chance to be your guy."

I considered what he said for a moment before replying. "Okay."

"Okay you'll go out with me?"

I nodded. "I'd love that."

"Really? Because you can say no. I don't want you to feel obligated or anything. We can just be friends."

I took his hands in mine and smiled. "I mean it. I just wish you had asked me sooner. It's going to suck not seeing you over break." Thinking about it more I added, "Well, we can probably meet up. You don't live very far. Are your parents picking you up tomorrow too?"

He shook his head and opened the door to the library. I followed him inside and we sat on a squashy couch across from a gas fireplace, just a few feet away from the librarian with the bad perm. The heat thawed my frozen fingers, and soon I was able to take off the gloves that he had lent me. I tossed them onto the armrest and slid closer to his side of the couch. I pulled him close to me, letting him know that it was okay to cuddle. Once we were fully settled, he circled back to my question.

"My parents are going to Arizona to visit my cousins. They said the flight was too expensive for me to tag along, but that I can spend Christmas with my Aunt Judy if I want to. I fucking hate Aunt Judy. She goes on these hour long tangents that don't make any sense and then calls me stupid."

The librarian looked up from her desk and scowled, presumably because of his foul language. Her pencil-drawn eyebrows twitched as she wagged a bony finger at him. A second wag and we'd be thrown out of there.

I waved to her sarcastically once she returned to reading *Paradise Lost.* "So if you aren't going there, then what are you doing? Not staying here I hope."

"Fuck no." The librarian looked up again and he twisted his face into a fake apologetic expression. "Excuse me ma'am. I meant to say heck no."

She shook her head disapprovingly, and took a sip of her coffee. It left an ugly brown stain on her upper lip, accentuating the hair that she had failed to wax.

Pat continued. "I'm not sure what I'm going to do yet. I'll probably just swing home and chill."

At first I thought that this was the coolest way to spend break. I imagined the freedom of spending break all alone, having the ability to do whatever you want whenever you wanted. But then I thought of how I usually spent the holidays: at home eating batch after batch of Christmas cookies while my mom whipped up a feast for dinner. She'd pretend like it was a burden and threaten that one day she was going to turn over the cooking to me. But everyone knew how much she loved doing it, and that she would continue to do it until the Grim Reaper came and dragged her out of the kitchen. Even then, we were sure she'd put up such a fuss about leaving that he'd have to wait until after the meal.

"Why don't you come home with me for break?" I asked.

Pat's eyes widened. "Would your parents be ok with that?"

"Of course," I lied.

There was no way that they'd actually be ok with it. Pat was the exact opposite of the type of guy they wanted me hanging around with. But that didn't mean that they wouldn't let him stay. One of the perks of living under a "good" Christian roof was that my parents felt sorry for people who had nowhere to go. If I told them that Pat's family had abandoned him during their favorite time of the year, they might let him stay. The only catch is that I couldn't let them know about Pat and I's new relationship status. Any hint of a romance and he'd be out the door before they could say, "No sex before marriage."

I relayed my conditions to Pat, and he reluctantly agreed to keep things under wraps. He removed his arm from around my shoulders and kissed me gently on the forehead. My cheeks flushed scarlet and he kissed them both.

"Why don't you give your folks a call to let them know I'll be joining you all? I wouldn't want to spring this on them tomorrow morning," he suggested.

"Sounds like a plan," I said getting up. I headed to the payphone that was adjacent to the restrooms, my head dizzy as I replayed the last few minutes over and over again. I dug through my pockets for change. The coins stuck to my hands before tumbling onto the floor. Eventually I managed to slide a dime into the slot, and shakily dialed my home number.

As it rang, I swore at my body for acting so stupidly. I had known Pat for months. There was no need to get all nervous now that we were a couple. Still, something had changed since we agreed to be more than friends. Now we would be getting to know each other in entirely new ways, ways that I had never gotten to know anyone before. Suddenly I felt as though no matter how close we were, we could never be close enough. I even missed him just standing there waiting to get off the phone. Were all people this neurotic at the beginning of a relationship?

"Hello?" my Mom answered, her voice nasally and her usual formality dropped.

"Hey mom, it's me. Do you have a cold?" I feigned concern. She was always catching colds from the Q-tip heads at church. It seemed that their devotion to God didn't do anything to boost their immune systems.

"Oh June! It's so good to hear from you. What time would you like us to pick you up tomorrow?"

"Ummm…" I twirled my fingers around the chord, "Is nine-ish good?"

"That's perfect. We'll be home before lunch! I'll make macaroni and cheese. You still eat that right? What with that new vegetarianism, I don't know what to make you. Your dad says it's just a phase...I really hope he's right."

I rolled my eyes. When I went home for Thanksgiving last month, he served me a big slab of turkey breast and insisted that I could use the extra protein. He had a hard time believing that anyone can get by on just veggies alone, even though I was healthier than ever. I tossed the meat back on the platter without comment, and took another helping of butter beans.

"Mom?" I asked when she was through with her little rant.

"Yes, honey?"

"I have a friend who doesn't have a place to go for the holidays. Do you think they can stay with us?"

The sound of an aluminum pan being banged against a countertop reverberated through the phone line. Evidently, she was in the middle of making one of her famous Bundt cakes. The trouble was they weren't famous for turning out well.

"What was that dear?" More banging followed by a muffled, "Oh for Pete's sake!" I waited patiently for her to remember that she was still talking to me as she banged, scraped, and ran her tin under cold water. "Sorry about that sweetie. Would you believe I forgot to grease the mold? Why, I've never done such as silly thing in all my life. What am I supposed to do with all these crumbs? It's a disaster!"

"I don't know, Mom."

"Well," she paused. "Maybe I can make a trifle. What was it you wanted to ask me?"

I cleared my throat. Waiting for her to finish playing Betty Crocker had done nothing to ease my anxiety. "Can my friend stay with us during break? They don't have anywhere to go."

She paused. "I'll have to ask your father, but I don't see why not. Not a soul in the world deserves to be alone on Christmas. We'll just have to change the sheets in the spare room so that they're nice and fresh. What is your friend's name?"

"Pat," I said slowly.

"Pat? What a lovely name. Short for Patricia I bet. Just like your great grandmother."

"What? No Mom—"

"—You tell Pat that she has nothing to worry about. We'll pick her up tomorrow the same time as you. It'll be nice to meet one of your friends. Your father and I didn't think you had any."

"Mom, Pat isn't short for Patricia it's—"

She turned on the sink and ran her pan under water again. "Sweetie I've got to go. This trifle isn't going to make itself. I'll be there before you know it to bring you and your friend home. Okay?"

I sighed. There was no point talking to her when she was like this. She'd have to find out Pat's true identity the hard way.

"Looking forward to it," I said.

"Wonderful. Goodnight Juniper. Sleep tight."

"Goodnight, Mom. I love you."

"I love you too sweetie."

Chapter 9: December 14th, 1968

The Pontiac rolled into campus at quarter to nine. Pat and I were waiting outside talking and smoking cigarettes before they arrived. Well, more accurately, *he* was smoking. It took a lot of effort not to join in, given how nervous I was for him to meet my 'rents. I had warned him that it might be a while before he got to smoke once my parents were in the picture. They considered cigarettes to be a gateway drug to hell, and he had promised to be on his best behavior.

As part of this promise, he had tried to dress semi-normally. He had traded his fringed vest and sandals for a cardigan and loafers. His face had been shaved so that it was as smooth as glass. His hair was still tousled and his undershirt tie-dyed but, compared to me, he looked like a million bucks.

When my parents got out of the car, they slowly walked over, eyeing the two of us carefully.

"Hi honey," my mom said approaching me. She pulled me into a swift hug and kissed me on each cheek. I thought about how different her affection felt from Pat's; the stark contrast between romance and familial obligation. She stood back and stared blatantly at Pat, as though he were a criminal. He quickly looked down at his feet. "Do you know this gentleman?" she asked, nodding towards him.

I opened my mouth to respond, but Pat extended a hand. "Good Morning Mrs. Carter. My name is Pat. I've heard so many great things about you. Thank you for inviting me to your home for the holidays. I really don't know where else I would've gone."

My mom shook his hand, trying her best not to look too stunned. Likely she had expected him to communicate using grunts and cuss words. Maybe she thought he'd steal her purse. That would have explained why she was clutching it so tightly.

My father shook his hand also, and began a conversation about the crash of Pan Am Flight 217 that had occurred two days prior. Once they had exhausted this topic, they discussed the upcoming inauguration of President Nixon.

Seeing that they were distracted, my mom pulled me aside.

"Juniper May Carter, you did *not* tell me that Pat is a boy." She dug her heels into the mushy grass and it made a fart noise as she lifted them out of the mud.

"I tried Mom, but you weren't listening. Anyway, he's a real nice guy. I promise he won't cause any trouble."

"Oh I don't know June…"

I guided her off of the grass and back onto the sidewalk. Her heels were definitely ruined from the muck. "Please, Mom. He's the only friend I've got. And we already told him he could stay. It would be rude to go back on our offer."

She took another look at him and sighed. "And you're sure he's not some sort of a heathen or something?"

"Mom! Thou shalt not judge, remember?"

"Thou shalt judge if it means protecting her family from riff-raff."

"He's not riff-raff. He's perfectly harmless. Give him a chance to prove himself. May I remind you that he has no where to go? No one should be alone on Christmas."

"Fine," she huffed, twisting her mouth into a false smile. She walked over to Pat and linked her arm around his as she said in her most polite voice possible, "We are happy to have you, Pat. Tell me, will you be attending church with us throughout your stay?"

Evidently, my father was slow to catch on. His face contorted with both shock and fear as he processed the identity of the person standing before him. My mom shot him a look that very clearly said, "I'll tell you later," and he returned to acting pleased by Pat's company.

"Yes ma'am. I'm looking forward to it," Pat said, winking in my direction.

I mouthed, "Sorry," but he waved me off. We stashed our luggage in the trunk and pulled out of the parking lot, wondering what we had gotten ourselves into.

My house was a Sears catalog home, built in 1916 for a thousand dollars. My grandparents had purchased it when my mom was eleven, and eventually gifted it to her as a wedding present. She made her own mark on it, painting it yellow instead of white and adding robin egg shutters. The inside looked like it had come straight out of a magazine. My mom made it a point to purchase new furniture every couple of years before the old furniture had the chance to go out of style. This annoyed me when I was smaller. I was sentimental about everything from the chocolate milk stain on the carpet to the cookie crumbs that had settled in the cracks of the couch, beyond the reach of my mom's vacuuming. By the time I was older, I thought it was kind of cool that our home was an ever-evolving reflection of our rapidly changing society. Evidently, Pat did too.

"Shit, this place is nice." He said, looking around the living room. We had already unpacked our bags and my mom was in the kitchen preparing lunch. My dad had followed her to read the newspaper at the table, leaving us to ourselves. Every now and then she poked her head around the corner to make sure that we weren't making babies.

Pat took a seat on the couch and bounced up and down, admiring its springy navy cushions and solid structure. I watched his eyes dart from the smooth coffee table with angled brass legs to the geometric tapestry behind the television. I wondered how my house compared to the place he had grown up in, but thought better than to ask. I knew that his folks weren't too well off.

When we were first getting to know each other, I asked him where he got all his money from. How was it that he was able to afford records and clothing and college tuition? Did his parents send him an allowance like mine did? Had his grandparents left him a hefty inheritance when they passed?

He got really quiet and explained that he had been earning his keep since he was old enough to walk by doing various odd-jobs around the neighborhood. His favorite task was taking care of people's pets while they were out of town. The one that brought him the most shame was stealing booze from his neighbors and selling it to his friends. That's how he had gotten so good at lock picking, from breaking into houses and tricky liquor cabinets.

As he got older it was harder to find work on account of his eccentric appearance and strong values. People no longer trusted him now that hair covered his half-moon ears and his once chubby cheeks became stubbled. Fortunately for him, by then it didn't matter. He had saved enough money to get by, having refused to indulge in childhood delights such as bubble gum and clothing that hadn't come from the thrift shop.

Now if he wanted a little extra spending cash, he played his guitar in parks and other well populated areas until the fuzz shooed him away. At least, that's what he did up until a month ago. He seemed to have taken a hiatus from music, one that I hoped would soon end. Now that we were a couple, I kind of hoped that he'd write a song about me.

Pat leaned over to the side table and snatched a frame from it. "Who's this?" he jeered. He didn't have to show it to me for me to know who it was a picture of, and why he was so amused.

It was a photo of me in high school sporting a skimpy pleated skirt and a sweater embellished with our school's hideous mascot: a red eagle. In it I was waving a set of oversized pom-poms and smiling. It wasn't one of those fake smiles that

122

politicians wore, but a real, goofy one that verged on ugly. I had been unsuccessfully trying to hide this photograph from my mother for the last three years. One time I hid it on the bookshelf in the attic. Another I buried it in the backyard. Somehow she always found it and put it back on display for everyone to see.

"Give me that," I said lunging for it.

He dodged my advances then sprang up and across the room. "I didn't know that you were a cheerleader," he said. "Nice pigtails."

"Seriously, Pat. Put it down." I begged. I ran towards him but he wrapped his arms around me tightly. I struggled to break free, annoyed by how strong he was. How could someone so lanky have such a firm grip? Were his muscles hidden in his hair? Eventually I allowed my body to melt into his and he let me go. He handed me the picture and I tossed it onto the rug, hard enough to show I meant business, but not hard enough to break the frame.

"There's no need to get upset," he said with his hands held up, "I was just busting your chops. Everyone has a past. So what if you were a cheerleader?"

He bent over and picked the picture up off of the ground before returning it to its proper place. The scent of melted cheese and boiled noodles wafted in from the other room, making our stomachs rumble loudly. I rubbed mine, shaking my head.

"I hate who I was back then. I was a total flake."

Pat looked confused. "You looked pretty happy to me."

"That's just the thing; I was. I didn't think anything was wrong with the way that I was living my life. Actually, I rarely thought at all. I just did what everyone told me to do. Go to school. Join cheerleading. Attend Bible study. In one activity I was taught to love others, in the other I chopped them down."

"You were just a teen," Pat said. "Don't be so hard on yourself."

"I was old enough to know better," I said.

He squeezed my hand consolingly. "No, you really weren't. But what made you change?"

My breath quickened. "Sophomore year my brother enlisted in the army—"

"—I didn't know you have a brother" he interjected.

I nodded. "I did. I was proud of him when he left. Can you believe that? *Proud*, because that's how everyone told me to feel. They claimed that he was saving our country."

I led Pat over to the shelf above the fireplace and retrieved a pocket-sized journal hidden behind a vase. It was leather-bound with worn seams; the only item in the living room to show any real signs of age. Several pages stuck out of it that were stained from weather, war, and who knows what else. Engraved on it was "Property of Joseph C. Carter."

I handed it to Pat, who held it with the same care that one uses when balancing an egg on a spoon. He began flipping through its contents, only stopping once he had reached the final entry: a goodbye note addressed to me. I told him that shortly after writing it, my brother had stolen some booze, snuck away from camp, and taken his own life. The army didn't bother sending us his body. They could only identify him by his teeth.

Pat tried to meet my eyes but I quickly looked away, pretending to be fascinated by the wood beams above me. When the silence between us became uncomfortable, I spoke barely above a whisper.

"After he died and I read his journal, I became horrified with the world that we live in, and the world that my family and friends had built for me. What hurt me the most was when I realized that my brother never had a chance at coming home. Not really. Even if he had made it out of there alive, he wouldn't have been the same boy we had always known. I spent weeks pouring through his nightmarish account of Vietnam: accounts of children being murdered and women being raped. I nearly drove myself mad reading and re-reading the last page, trying to make sense of it. When I was too tired to analyze it any further I skipped school for a solid week to sleep. My parents thought that I had the flu...

"...Not long after that I decided to stop being so ignorant. To really observe things as they are and to form my own opinions about them, just like my brother did towards the end of his life. I'm really proud of how far I've come. But I still have a lot of work to do. Seeing that picture of me from before all that happened makes me afraid that I'll slip back into being the person I no longer want to be. I guess that's why I didn't want you to see that picture. I didn't want you, of all people, to know the old me."

Pat sighed. "June, who you are is the sum of who you once were. Don't ever think you have to hide your past. Not from me, not from anyone. Do you understand?"

I opened my mouth to respond but was interrupted by my mother who had flounced into the room. She pouted when she saw her son's diary in Pat's hand, and Pat quickly returned it to where it belonged.

"Lunch is ready," she croaked, "Mac and cheese and strawberry gelatin to boot. I hope you're hungry."

Pat crossed the room and gently pressed my mom's arm. Her face creased with sadness and surprise, but she didn't seem bothered by his touch.

"I'm real sorry for your loss Mrs. Carter," he said.

"Thank you, Pat." She was peering everywhere but at him. Now I knew where I had picked up the habit. Carter girls weren't ones to cry in front of others, and once we got going it was difficult to stop. The easiest way to avoid doing it was to retreat into ourselves for a moment or two, willing the tears to go back to where they came from. If that didn't work, we fled.

My mom patted her apron and pinned on a weary smile. "You guys go on into the kitchen and get it while it's hot. Just save me a bowl of each and wash up when you're done."

"Yes ma'am," Pat said, as my mom slid by him.

I heard the familiar clomping of her heels against wood as she went up the stairs and into her room to pray. She slammed the door behind her, causing the ceramic cross in the stairwell to fall on the floor, and then split in half.

Pat cupped his hand over his ears and knelt down.

I laughed, thinking he was messing around. "She's so dramatic isn't she? She's going to be pissed when she sees what she did. My grandmother gave her that cross right before she died. It's been in the family for decades."

He returned to a standing position and looked around like he was expecting someone to jump out from behind the curtains and yell "Boo."

"Hey, are you alright?" I asked.

He nodded slowly, crossing his arms tightly in front of him.

"Are you cold or something?"

He shivered. "Yeah, that's probably it."

I went into the hall closet and retrieved a blanket for him. He wrapped it around himself, still looking disturbed.

"Why don't you go ahead and start lunch?" I asked. "I'm going to go see if my dad can glue the cross together."

"Alright," Pat said, peering around once more.

By the time that I joined him in the kitchen, he was back to his usual self.

Chapter 10: December 24th, 1968

"Look, June. It's snowing."

Pat was sitting at the kitchen table gazing out at the backyard. Snow flurries swirled through the air like powdered sugar being sifted over a fresh batch of donuts. They landed gracefully on the lawn and layered themselves one on top of the other until they resembled a wool blanket.

"Beautiful," I said coming to his side. I handed him a spoonful of cookie dough from the next batch of sweets, and his focus turned to cleaning the utensil one lick at a time. When he finished, I threw it in the baking bowl that was soaking in the sink, and checked on the gingerbread.

I opened the oven and the aroma of cinnamon, allspice, and cloves filled the air. The cookies were maple brown with dark edges and ready to come out. I barely had a chance to set them on the counter to cool before Pat came up behind me and stole one off of the tray. He stood there with his mouth open, fanning it and complaining that they were too hot. I whacked him with the oven mitt and yelled at him for being stupid. He no sooner swallowed it before shoving another one into his mouth.

"For Christ's sake. Do you even have any taste buds left?"

He had done the same thing with the snicker-doodles, peanut butter, and sugar cookies that I had prepared earlier. It was a wonder he hadn't suffered third degree burns or gone into a sugar coma.

He stuck out his tongue to show me that they were still in tact. "Can we make pecan sandies next?" he asked as I scrubbed the dishes.

I raised an eyebrow. "You mean can *I* make pecan sandies?"

He laughed, taking the washcloth from me.

I switched places with him so that he could take over cleaning duty.

"Hey, I help. I make sure that the cookies aren't poisoned so that the good people of St. Whoever's church will have something delicious to eat." He rinsed the baking bowl then handed it to me to dry. "What time do we have to be there anyway?"

I grabbed a fresh towel and mopped up the water that remained at the bottom of the dish. "Mass begins at midnight, but the cookie exchange is in the basement at nine."

"And why are we going to that again?"

"It's a tradition. Besides, would you really want to pass up the opportunity to sample dozens of cookies? They've got to be one of your favorite foods."

He washed the spoon that he had licked earlier and handed it to me. I handed it back, pointing to a chocolate chip that needed to be washed off. Upon closer inspection, I returned the bowl he had just "cleaned" to the sink as well.

He took it without complaint. "Hell no. I just thought cookie exchanges were for old people and stay at home moms, not two youngsters like us. And for your information, they *are* my favorite food. No contest."

I twisted the towel and gently whipped him with it. "It's a wonder you don't throw up, you know that?"

He grinned. "Hey, I didn't say that I don't feel sick. But as soon as I upchuck these babies, I'll have room for more."

I wrinkled my nose and kicked the trash can towards him. Within minutes he was filling it with half digested Christmas cookies. When he finished I cracked open a bottle of ginger ale and encouraged him to sip it while I hid the sweets from view. He thanked me and downed the whole thing before going into the guest room to lie down.

In the meantime I took out the trash, doing my best not to think of the bag's contents. There was a reason why my parents had never expected me to become a nurse. One glance at vomit and I contributed more fluids to the mess. I suspect that the only reason I didn't toss my own cookies right then and there was because I loved Pat.

I knew that it was frowned upon to say the "L" word too early in a relationship, so I didn't say anything to him about how I felt. But if the way that I felt about him didn't count as love, I didn't want any part of it. Having him stay with me and the folks over Christmas break had only confirmed what I already knew. Pat was everything that the world needed more of, all rolled into one being. I doubted that anyone like that could feel the same about me. I wasn't perfectly imperfect like him. Even when he drove me nuts he made up for it by being my favorite person.

Just yesterday my mom took the two of us into town for a little last minute Christmas shopping. She went off to buy me one final present, leaving Pat and me to roam the streets by ourselves. Almost as soon as she left, Pat whipped out a cigarette and lit it.

"Put that thing out," I said looking over my shoulder. My mom was just beyond the door, chatting with the shopkeeper.

Pat ignored me and continued to smoke, puffing out cancer clouds with pleasure. "Chill out, June. I haven't smoked since last night when they went out for dinner. I'm dying here."

"She could come out of the store at any moment," I said. "If she catches you smoking you're toast. We both are."

Pat pointed behind us. Mom was being lead to the back of the store by a thin woman in uniform. I knew that this meant I'd be receiving a pair of stockings for Christmas. The back of the store was where they kept more nylon than was used by the troops in World War II. I only hoped that my other gifts would be more exciting.

We crossed the street and walked down the sidewalk in silence. He was too busy enjoying the cigarette and fresh air to be bothered with conversation, and I was too annoyed with him to speak.

A woman with a dirty coat and a frayed scarf approached us. She carried a silver tin in her blistered, purple hands. I looked down to avoid staring into her eyes, which were cloudy with cataracts. I wanted to pass by as quickly as possible, pretending not to notice her, but Pat had other plans. He paused directly in front of her and wished her a Merry Christmas.

"And a Merry Christmas to you sir," she exclaimed. Her voice suggested that she was much younger than she appeared. Being out in the elements had a way of doing that to people. She gave us a toothy grin. "I'm raising money for the Homeless Shelter just a few blocks away from here. Could I interest either of you in a cake in exchange for a small donation?"

"No th—" I began, eager to get away, but Pat interrupted me.

"Right on," he said, searching for his wallet. He took out a crisp dollar bill and handed it to her. She quickly put it in the pouch that was dangling around her waist. She handed him his lumpy dessert and thanked him profusely.

"God bless you, young man! God bless!" she hollered even after we were gone.

He put up a peace sign and returned the sentiment. My anger towards him swiftly transformed into admiration. We found the nearest bench and ate the cake with our bare hands. It was the best one I had ever had.

A couple of hours went by and Pat had yet to come back down stairs. I figured that he had fallen asleep, so I went into the living room to read. My mom was already there re-arranging the ornaments on the Christmas tree for the thousandth time, while my dad fussed with the television antennas.

By the time Pat emerged, it was just minutes before we had to leave for church. My mom gave him a once over, shaking her head. "You aren't wearing *that* to church, are you?"

Pat looked taken aback, "No disrespect ma'am, but I wasn't sure what to wear. I didn't bring much with me."

"I see." Her mouth became a thin line as she disappeared around the corner. When she came back she was carrying a freshly pressed suit and tie, which I recognized as my brother's. My brother had reluctantly worn it the Christmas before he went off to war, complaining all the while that it made him look like an elderly preacher. My mom told him to hush and be grateful that the good lord had blessed him with such fine clothing. He spent the whole night pretending to be old, giving unwanted advice and starting most of his sentences with the phrase "Youngins these days."

My mother had been so embarrassed by my brother that I had expected her to throw the suit out. Never in my wildest dreams did I think she would not only keep it, but continue to launder it. Yet here she was, pushing it into Pat's arms while he smiled politely. It was even uglier than I remembered it.

He came out of the bathroom looking just as my brother had: uncomfortable yet entertained by just how bad it was.

"You look marvelous," Mom said. "It fits like a glove." Tugging at the waist she added, "Well, maybe he had a bit more meat on his bones than you do. He wasn't one of those vegetarians like you are. But it's not bad, not bad at all. What do you think, Juniper?"

I nodded in fake approval. "It's a sight to see, that's for sure."

Satisfied, she ushered us into the kitchen to gather the cookies.

Pat and I trailed behind and I whispered in his ear, "*I think that it's a good thing you have a cute face or I'd break up with you.*"

"What?" he asked sarcastically, "Not a fan of my new suit? I was going to ask if she'd let me keep this little number."

"Shut up," I said a little too loudly. My mother whipped her head around at us.

"Juniper! Watch your mouth. That is no way for a young lady to speak, let alone to a man."

"Sorry."

She loaded our arms with stacks of orange Tupperware each containing several dozen cookies. Our piles were so high that neither of us could see over them. We had to crane our heads around them so that we wouldn't collide with one another. My dad avoided coming into the kitchen, not wanting to carry anything but his keys. My mom grabbed her coat and gloves, then said something about being on door duty. Pat and I placed as much of our loot as we could fit into the trunk while the rest of it sat on our laps for the ride.

We arrived at the church in record time. I suspect that my dad was eager to drop us off so that he would no longer fall victim to my mom's nonstop gossip. No, he didn't know that Mrs. Johnson was a cheap tipper or that Mary-Ann's daughter got knocked up by her jobless boyfriend and was now living with an aunt up in Canada. Frankly, he didn't give a damn unless the words "Super Bowl" were involved.

Our church was a brick building with milky window frames and a mint-colored door. The door had been painted by some teenagers several years ago who had intended it as a prank, but the priest liked it so much, he decided to keep it.

We were greeted at the door by Ms. Eleanor, a quaint old lady wearing more jewelry than her tiny frame could manage without hunching over.

"Good evening Ms. Eleanor," my mother said, kissing her once on each cheek. She hesitated a moment before adding, "My, I've never seen so many necklaces all worn at once. You must be setting some sort of record."

Ms. Eleanor stroked them. "Macy's was having a sale and I just couldn't resist. They're so elegant, don't you think?"

My mom faked a smile. It looked like she had just come back from having a Botox injection. "Oh they're something else. By the by, have you met Patrick? He's staying with us through the holidays, and has been a right pleasure to have."

Pat placed his pile of Tupperware on the ground so that he could shake Ms. Eleanor's hand.

"Wonderful." She said. "You have a good firm grip, just like a man should have. And such nice eyes, just like a movie star. No wonder June snatched you up."

My mom interrupted her. "—Oh no Ms. Eleanor, he's just a friend of the family." In her tartest voice possible she added, "It would be inappropriate to invite a boyfriend to stay the holidays, don't you think? Especially one that her parents wouldn't approve of."

Pat's lips curled into a snarl but he quickly changed his face to a more pleasant expression.

Ms. Eleanor didn't bother to hide her disgust and said, "I think any young lady would be lucky to have such a gentleman. What do you have to say on the matter June?"

The Tupperware containers trembled beneath my chilled hands. If I responded honestly, my mom might become suspicious of our relationship and ask questions later on. But if I didn't respond at all, Pat would be hurt, and he didn't deserve that.

"Pat already has a girlfriend, and she thinks he's great," I said at last. I hoped that this response would satisfy everyone.

My mom narrowed her eyes, and Pat struggled to hide his smirk. Ms. Eleanor winked at me, indicating that she knew the truth of the situation. Somehow, she always did. It was a relief to have someone else know that we were a couple, even if it was only the town's crazy lady.

"I wasn't aware of this," my mom said, interrupting my thoughts. Composing herself she added, "Well, good for you I guess. You know what they say; there's a lid for every pot. I just hope that my Juniper finds her lid before she's all cracked and misshapen."

"Really mom?"

"What? It's true. If you don't start using that night cream I got you, you'll have wrinkles before you're twenty. No man wants to marry a woman with wrinkles, honey. Isn't that right, Pat?"

A man in a brown suit mounted the steps, excusing himself for interrupting our conversation. He pulled open the door and held it for us, insisting that we go in before we catch a cold. We thanked him and entered the church, which was noisy from the click-clack of women's heels and excited chatter. I closed my eyes, breathing in the familiar scent of beeswax mingling with floral perfume and baby powder.

The cookie swap went about as well as expected. Mom floated from pack to pack of women, listening in on their conversations and filing away every juicy tidbit to spread later on.

Pat sampled dozens of cookies ranging from thumbprints to

walnut, then threw them all up so that he could sample some more.

I stuck close to him whenever I could, but was often stolen away

by family friends who wanted updates on how I was enjoying

college. Some of them talked about their grandsons and insisted on

giving me their phone numbers. Others tried persuading me that

college was no place for a woman. They still thought of me as the

cheerleader from high school, only capable of being somebody's

wife. The idea of me getting an education genuinely worried them.

At a quarter to midnight we headed to mass. Quietly we

slid into the second pew from the front, reserved for frequent

donors. As we waited for mass to start, Pat bounced his legs up and

down shaking the whole thing. My mom glared at him.

"Quit it," I whispered into his ear. "Are you nervous or

something?"

He nodded and grabbed one of the Bibles from the shelf on

the back of the pew. He flipped through the pages, his eyes darting

back and forth, taking in some passages, ignoring others. It looked

like he was cramming for a test, a skill most college kids had already mastered that he had never used. I wondered why he was so shaken, and guessed that he had never stepped foot in a church before now. Or, maybe he had, and was bothered by the whole idea of religion.

The priest came in and Pat quickly put the book away. He tucked his hair behind his ears which were growing red, and smoothed his pants. He listened intently as the priest spoke, like a child being told a bedtime story. I wondered what thoughts were spiraling through his galaxy of a brain, a realm more mysterious and complex than a black hole. He sang when we were invited to sing, and prayed when we were told to pray. When the time came to accept our holy communion, Pat was the first to stand from our row, but the last to receive his wine, wafer, and blessing. I wasn't sure if this was allowed, because he never told me if he was confirmed. But nobody stopped him, and he didn't turn into ash on the spot.

When the ceremony was over, Pat and I went out into the hall while my mom lingered behind to talk with the priest. She and a few others had made a habit of doing this every time they attended church. I referred to them as God's Groupies and offered to make them t-shirts. My mother wasn't the slightest bit amused by this nickname.

Pat's good behavior ended shortly after the service. He splashed holy water on his forehead from a stone bath by the doors then pulled a cigarette out of his pocket and lit it. Passerby shot him looks of disapproval. I quickly cradled my arm through his and escorted him out of the church and onto the freshly-shoveled sidewalk. I unbuttoned my coat, warm despite the frigid temperature and the snow that was swirling around us.

"June, do you think there's a God?' Pat asked, nervously.

I blinked, surprised that he'd ask such a question. He and I had never talked religion before, other than to discuss the people who used it as an excuse to run other people's lives. I looked around to make sure no one else had heard him.

"Well yeah," I hesitated. "Of course I do. Don't you?"

Pat took a long drag of his cigarette and stared down at his shoes. I could see his mind battling with itself as it weaved in and out of dark places. He looked so fragile that I wanted to hug him, but I refrained. People were filing out of the church and getting into their shiny cars. My mom would be quick to join them once she fulfilled her obligations as priest's pet.

He stamped his cigarette into the pavement and shrugged. "I wanted to," he said finally. "I really, truly did."

I wanted to ask him what he meant by this, but my parents joined us outside. My mom sniffed the air and commented on the scent of tobacco that had clung to it. "How tacky of people to smoke on church grounds," she said. "Don't they know this is a holy space? Fire is for sinners, not for good Christians like us."

We collectively ignored her and made our way home, eager to get some shut eye.

Chapter 11: December 25th 1968

My brother and I were seated on the rug in front of the fireplace,

drinking mugs of hot chocolate with cinnamon sticks for straws.

Behind us was the couch, lime green with oversized pillows, the

same couch we had gotten rid of when I was in First Grade. On

our right was the Christmas tree, draped with thick layers of tinsel

and shiny pink bobbles, exactly as it had been before my brother

went off to war.

I knew that my brother was dead and that I was enjoying

the company of his ghost. Yet, him being there was the most

normal thing in the world. He asked me how I've been doing, and

whether Mom was still a handful. I asked him whether heaven lived

up to all the hype.

We took a sip of our hot chocolate as a log fell out of the fire. It rolled towards us, burning an oblong hole in the rug. My brother picked up the log with his bare hands, and returned it to the hearth. He placed a metal grate over the open flame to prevent it from tumbling out again. The flames glowed blue and then red before dying out. The room grew cold.

"I have to go," my brother said. "I'm due back."

I shivered. "So soon? Can't you at least finish your cocoa?"

He shook his head with a finality that couldn't be opposed.

I scooped him into a hug, not wanting him to leave. When he no longer felt solid, I was forced to let go.

He handed me his mug, then pointed towards a figure that stood in the threshold between the living room and the hallway. The figure was translucent, with disfigured hands and blurred features. It looked like it was between two worlds, not fully existing in either one. I feared it for a moment, and then felt sympathetic. Even with its marred face I recognized it as Pat.

"Keep an eye out on this one," my brother said walking towards him. He stuck an arm through Pat's body, but Pat didn't stir. "He's fading."

The wind howled, frightening me awake. I had kicked off my sheets in the night, and my hair was matted with sweat. I was pissed at myself for waking up. I had never dreamt of my brother or Pat before, and I wanted to see how things played out.

I rolled over and the clock read 3:00 a.m. on the dot. The wind continued its wretched reign, whipping the tree branches and creeping through the cracks in the window frame. I sat up and wrapped my blankets tightly around me, more chilled by my dream than the frigid temperature. It would be several more hours until anyone else would wake, hours that I didn't want to spend alone, playing and replaying the dream over and over again in my tired mind.

I got out of bed and tiptoed to the door. It groaned as it twisted open, so I squeezed my eyes tightly together, as though this would muffle the sound. I waited, listening for anyone stirring.

Convinced that I was the only one up, I continued my journey to Pat's room.

I entered as quietly as possible and hesitated in the doorway. His knees were curled tightly against his bare chest, which moved up and down slowly. He looked so handsome lying there, serene as the quarter moon that rested easy against the night sky. I debated turning around, satisfied that he was perfectly undisturbed. I'm not sure what I'd expected to see. Did I really think he'd be transparent like he was in my dream?

Instead I slid next to him, mimicking his sleeping position. He opened his eyes and kissed me softly, first on my temple, and then on my neck. He pulled me closer and kissed me once more on the shoulder. I traced his hands using my own, amazed by how beautiful they were. I was relieved to have him there, solid, the center of my world. Within minutes he drifted back to sleep and I followed closely behind, the dream a distant memory.

Morning came and we remained tangled in each other's arms from the night before. I was the first to wake, and ran my fingers through my hair to make it semi presentable. Bed-head didn't work for people as unsexy as I was. It worked really well for Pat though.

I watched Pat sleep for several minutes, dreading having to wake him from this blissful state. My parents would be up soon and the last thing that I wanted was for them to find me here, being spooned by him. But I also didn't want to leave without saying good morning.

"Hey, Pat," I said nudging him gently. "It's time to get up."

His eyes flickered open but I could tell that something was wrong. His irises were as grey as the snow-laden clouds outside. They were angry, sad and distant. They looked like they belonged to a man ten times his age.

"Get off of me," he said.

"What?" I asked. But he hadn't been talking to me. Not really.

"Get the fuck *off* of me!" he screamed. He rolled onto his back and threw his fists in the air, jabbing at an invisible enemy. His skin paled as sweat dripped down his arms and legs, soaking the sheets.

"Stop it Pat. It's just me, June. Your girlfriend," I said grasping his flailing hands, but he was too strong. He continued to flail like a bird with clipped wings, accidentally tossing me to the floor in the process. I landed with a loud *thud* and failed to contain my tears. It wasn't that the landing had hurt, though I was sure that my hip had been thoroughly bruised. It was the fact that he had been the one to cause the pain.

"June?" Pat peered over the mattress at me, having snapped out of whatever nightmare had gripped him. "Oh my God." He leaped onto the ground and examined me. "Are you hurt? Did I hurt you? What happened?" His eyes had returned to their natural state, but were wet with tears. He reached out to stroke my cheek but I swatted him away.

The door swung open and my mom stormed in.

"What on God's green earth is going on in here?" she yelled. She first looked at Pat who was straddling me, shirtless and out of breath. She then turned to me. I was crying and my pajama bottoms had ripped as I fell, exposing my right thigh. "Bob! Bob!" she shouted to my father. "Get in here, quick!"

Pat scrambled to his feet and helped me onto mine. He stared down at the floorboards awaiting my father's wrath while I tried reasoning with my mother.

"It isn't what it looks like. I came in to wake him up and tripped over the rug. He was just checking on me," I said.

My mom put her hands on her hips. "Juniper May Carter I wasn't born yesterday. Now tell me what really happened or I'm going to call the police and—" my dad entered the room, "—Oh there you are, Bob. Get him out of here."

My dad stepped forward, following his wife's instructions.

Pat stepped away from him. His eyes were becoming grey again, but instead of flipping out as he had earlier, he remained calm. He put on a shirt that was crumpled on the ground and then held my hand.

"What're you doing?" I whispered.

My mom's mouth hung open stupidly.

"Coming clean," he said, clenching his jaw. "Mr. and Mrs. Carter, your daughter and I are going steady. We have been since before I got here. I know you think she deserves better, but I'm not a bad guy. I promise to always do right by her, and to take myself out of the equation if I think I'm doing otherwise."

My mom closed her mouth, pressing her lips together until they were drained of color.

He continued, "I'm sorry we woke you up. Truth is, I was having a nightmare and June heard my shouting. She just came in here to see if I was okay. She tripped over the rug just like she said she did, and when you arrived I was making sure she wasn't injured. You folks just came in at a bad time."

My mother shook her head and fondled the gold cross that forever remained at the base of her neck.

"Is this true?" she asked with drowning eyes. "Are you seeing him?"

I nodded.

"*Leave*."

"What?"

"*Leave*, right this instant. I want you both out of my house by the count of three or I swear to the good lord that I'll...I'll" She broke down sobbing, as ugly as I ever saw. I hugged her and to my surprise, she didn't resist. She just fell into my arms like a sack of potatoes.

"Don't make her leave Mrs. Carter. I'll go," Pat said. "Just let her stay and go on with your Christmas like I was never here."

Mom wiped her nose with her silk pajama sleeve. Her eyes were gloopy from the mascara that she had forgotten to remove after mass, and her hair was sticking out at odd angles. She looked like a wet clown standing there in her grief. If I hadn't been so upset, I would have teased her about it.

Pat swiftly pecked my lips and whispered, "See you after break."

He raced down the stairs, not bothering to take his luggage with him. I ran after him despite my mom's icy glare.

"Don't go," I said. "I'm sure they'll cool off in a few hours. They wouldn't really kick you out on Christmas...at least I don't think they would. They love Christmas. It's Jesus's birthday for crying out loud."

He continued his descent but turned around once he reached the first floor. "It's fine, June. Just do me a favor and bring my bags with you when you return to school. They'll only weigh me down."

"Weigh you down? Where are you going?"

He shrugged, trying not to look as lost as he surely felt. "I think I'll walk until I'm tired and then try to hitch a ride."

"Okay…" I said slowly, "but where will you go?"

He shrugged again. "Does it matter? Don't worry about me. I'll be back at school by the time the holidays are over. I wouldn't leave you alone to deal with the clones." He pulled open the front door and a wave of cold air blew up the stairs. My toes turned purple upon impact.

"I'm coming with you," I said.

He shook his head. "No you aren't. I need to do this alone, and you need to stay here and patch things up with your parents."

Pat took his coat out of the hall closet and slid on his shoes. I was relieved that he at least intended to take this much on his journey.

"Are you sure you still want to be my girlfriend?" he asked. I had never seen him look as afraid as he did then. "Maybe us being together isn't such a great idea after all. Maybe you do deserve better."

"Of course I want to be your girlfriend. Nothing that my parents say can change that," I said. "Besides, they'll come around eventually. Just give them some time."

He pretended to smile. It was broken, but still handsome. I wished that he wouldn't go.

I climbed down the stairs and hugged him tightly. He released me too soon then stepped outside. I watched as he walked down the sidewalk, pulling a cigarette from his coat pocket. He glanced once over his shoulders and for a second I thought he might turn back. But he continued to walk until the only part of him that remained was his footprints in the snow.

Chapter 12: December 25th, 1968

Once Pat was out of sight, my mom and dad came downstairs and turned on the coffee maker. They didn't say anything to me, and I didn't say anything to them. I just sat on the living room sofa, wallowing in my anger while they whispered to one another in the kitchen. I couldn't hear what they were saying, but I didn't care. I figured that two people as judgmental as they were couldn't possibly have anything good to say. I just wished that they had chosen the living room to talk in so I could've claimed the kitchen. I would've killed for a cup of Earl Grey tea and a sugar cookie.

After they breakfasted, I heard my mom slide her chair out from underneath the table. She arrived with a dustpan and began cleaning as loudly as humanly possible. Of course, nothing actually needed cleaning. All she really did was move things around a little, and sigh a lot. I could tell she was trying to get me to apologize. Over the years I became convinced that she had single-handedly invented the silent treatment.

She swept up the few pine needles that were strewn across the floor before poking at the presents under the tree.

"I can't even begin to think of what to do with all of these presents," she said.

I took the bait. The sooner one of us stormed out of the room, the better. "What presents mom?"

"Well yours, of course. And..." she hesitated as though the next word was too offensive to say aloud, "Pat's."

I cocked my head. "Pat had presents?"

"Well of course he did. Everyone should get a present on Christmas. That is, everyone who deserves one. I'm not so sure that you fit that category anymore. Not after that stunt you pulled."

I shrugged, trying my best to appear unperturbed. My mom loved a good confrontation, especially when she thought she was on the winning side.

"It was nice of you to get him something," I said calmly. "But maybe you should just donate whatever you bought us."

She fondled her cross necklace. "You mean it doesn't bother you that you aren't getting anything for Christmas?"

I shook my head. "Nope. I already got a Christmas gift. Pat and I exchanged at school, and it's the best present I ever received."

Her eye twitched. "And what, may I ask, did he give you? Bugs perhaps?"

"Bugs?"

"Oh I can only imagine all of the critters crawling around in that hair of his. It's disgusting." She shivered.

I banged my fist against the side table. The photo from my cheerleading days toppled over. "That's not fair," I screeched. "There's nothing wrong with his hair. I like it."

"Not fair? Did you think it was fair to keep the fact that you had a boyfriend a secret from me? Or to bring him home for the holidays? I've never heard of such a thing. It's obscene!"

I paused. "No I guess not...but..."

She continued, "Why of all the ways to embarrass me, this has to be the lowest. All I've ever done is been a good mother to you, yet you continue to find new ways to push my buttons."

"What?" I shouted. "Is that what you think I was doing? Oh my God, mom. You just have to make everything about you, don't you? Did it ever cross your mind that I did this one thing for me? Or that I love him?"

She threw her hands up into the air. "Don't use the lord's name in vain. I might not have the power to damn you, but he sure can."

"Damn me for dating Pat? How can you say that after meeting him? He's been nothing short of amazing this whole break. Maybe you're the one that should be damned."

My mom dropped the dustpan, sending pine needles everywhere. "You take that back Juniper Carter."

I stood up so that we were at eye level. "Make me."

If looks could kill, I would've been dead and buried.

"Go to your room. I can't stand to look at you anymore,' she said.

"Funny, I was thinking the same thing." I bounded up the steps and into my room. I grabbed a brush off of my dresser and threw it at the wall, narrowly avoiding my mirror. I picked it up off the floor and then flopped onto my bed and sobbed. It wasn't that I was sorry for what I had said. Actually, I was pissed. Pissed at my mom for being such a stuck-up bitch, and pissed at myself for crying because of it.

When I was all cried out, my mind swelled with the things that I should've said, followed by ideas as to what I should do next. Each new idea was crazier than the last. Should I sneak out and try to find Pat? Should I stay there, in bed, refusing meals until I died? Or become a vagabond?

Knock Knock. Someone rapped on the door softly.

"Go away. I'm not in the mood."

The knob twisted and I swore under my breath. I had forgotten to lock the damn thing.

"What are you deaf? I asked. "Go away."

My dad entered the room, hunched over and fidgeting with his collar. The last time he was in there was when I was eight. My doll's head had fallen off, and he came up to repair it. Afterwards he fashioned a neck brace out of packing peanuts and blue thread, then instructed me to leave it on for a few days while she healed. I thought it was so cool that I never took it off. All of my friends had been jealous of it.

My room had changed a lot since then, and so had I. I don't think that he realized the extent of these changes until right then. He looked gloomy, standing there, staring at me. The girl he no longer knew. For a second I felt guilty for the woman I had grown into. Just for a second though.

"Mind if I sit down?" he asked, gesturing toward my desk.

"I guess not."

He dragged the chair over so that it was facing me. "Your mom is really upset you know."

"I know."

"By the looks of it, so are you."

No shit Sherlock.

"Mhhm."

My dad leaned forward and held my forearm awkwardly. I patted it, hoping he'd back off, thinking he had succeeded in comforting me. I wasn't used to being in such close proximity to him. It kind of creeped me out, but I knew he meant well.

"Do you really love this boy?" he asked solemnly.

My throat became tight. "Yes, I do."

"Alright then."

"What's that supposed to mean?" I asked.

He smiled. I could count on one hand how many times I'd seen him do that. "It means I can't stop you from loving him, and that I believe he'll take care of you." He paused, observing me.

The tears were now rolling freely down my cheeks, and I didn't try to stop them. He passed me his blue handkerchief and I snotted it up.

He continued, "At first when I learned that you're going out with Pat, I was ready to kill him. He's not the sort of guy I always imagined for my little girl. But then I realized that you're not the girl I imagined. You're much, much different than you once were. You don't need your mom and me telling you who to love or how to live your life. You've got your mind all made up. I see that now. It isn't an easy pill for a parent to swallow."

I blew once more into his snot rag which was now soggy.
There was no way he'd want it back, so I put it on my side table.
"If only mom could be as cool with us being together as you are.
She'll never accept our relationship. She's too stubborn."

He chuckled, "June, where do you think your stubbornness
comes from?"

"Shit. I'm just like her, aren't I?" I pressed my palms
against my cheeks and rubbed my temples.

"Watch your mouth young lady."

"Sorry."

"I'll overlook it." He checked his watch. By now mom
would be elbow deep in turkey guts, crying that next year we are
going out to eat.

"It's true that your mom will never be ok with you and
Pat," he said. "And I'm not saying that I am either. I've just
accepted that you might not marry a doctor or a lawyer, or one of
the nice boys from church. I'm afraid that's the best I can do."

"I appreciate that," I said.

He got up from his chair, and I stood too. I wrapped my
arms around his shoulders, and he hugged me with one arm. The

other arm hung limply at his side, as though he didn't know what to do with it.

My mom called out for him, saying something about needing help opening a can.

"Duty calls," he joked. "Why don't you get changed and come downstairs? It *is* Christmas after all."

"Yeah, that'd be nice," I said considering it. "Just as long as she promises not to mention Pat again today. I don't want to argue anymore."

"I think we can arrange that," he said.

I took my time getting changed then joined my parents in the kitchen. The turkey had only been in the oven for a few minutes, but it already smelled delicious. On days like this I missed eating meat, and worked hard to imagine the bird as it was alive, before its butt was stuffed with bread and its skin massaged with rosemary and butter.

When I sat down at the table, my mom was busy preparing a pumpkin pie. She nodded towards the fridge. "I made you a green bean casserole," she said stiffly. "I'll put it in before dinner so it'll be nice and hot, then I'll top it with those crispy onions you like so much. You like green beans right?"

I grinned. She had never made green bean casserole before, even though I had requested it on numerous occasions. I was the only one in my family who enjoyed the dish, so she considered it a waste of resources.

"Yeah I like green beans," I said. "Thanks a lot mom."

Her lips turned upward as she dusted the countertop with flour. She plopped a big ball of dough onto it and flattened it with my grandmother's wood rolling pin. She expertly shaped it into a circle then carefully set it in a pie dish greased with Crisco.

"Once this is in the oven, let's all go out into the living room to open our presents," she said. "Doesn't that sound like fun? I'll even have your father start a fire. That'll make it real cozy."

She crimped the edges of the dough, pulling off excess pieces so that she could shape them into holly as decorations for the top of the pie.

"That sounds really nice," I said. "I can't wait."

I hadn't forgiven her for the things she said about Pat, but the casserole was a damn good peace offering. After dealing with the clones all semester and worrying about Pat, I was tired of being

on guard all the time. I needed somewhere to retreat to that wasn't

volatile and for the time being, I'd have to make do with home.

Even if it meant getting along with my mom.

Chapter 13: January 12th, 1969

Spring semester began a week after the New Year, but Pat didn't show. At first I thought he was just skipping classes and that I'd find him in his dorm, at the radio station, or at the vegetarian restaurant in town. When a few days went by without a sighting of him, I started getting nervous. I had no way of contacting him. I had no address to send a letter to, and no phone number. For all I knew, he had been hit by car or murdered.

I hoped that he was happy wherever he was, even though I was kind of peeved. He *had* promised to be back in time for school, hadn't he? Pat wasn't the type of guy to go back on his word, but I wouldn't put it past him to walk off into the woods and get lost for good. He'd probably enjoy it out there with the trees and fresh air. The only thing he'd miss would be cigarettes, his guitar and hopefully me. Even then I figured he'd find a way to get by without us.

The Sunday that marked his second weekend MIA, I returned from a shower to find him lying on my bed. He had fallen asleep after coming in through the window that I left perpetually unlatched. My roommate wasn't there to yell at him for sneaking in. It turned out that she wasn't too happy with the college life, so she dropped out and got herself hitched. I have no idea how she found a husband so quickly. My guess is that she met someone equally as desperate as she was. The college hadn't gotten around to assigning a replacement roommate for me.

I crept up on Pat and jostled him awake, clutching my towel so that it wouldn't drop. His eyes fluttered open and he stared at the space where towels typically squeeze one's boobs together. He didn't seem bothered by the fact that mine were non-existent, and continued to stare until I cleared my throat loudly.

"Where were you?" I growled once I had his full attention.

He sat up and threw a pillow over his lap. "Oh, you know, everywhere and nowhere all at once."

I rolled my eyes at him and bent down, looking for something to throw on quick. I located a blouse and a pair of paisley pajama bottoms. I put them on quickly, not bothering to ask him to look away. I was too angry to care. "Either you tell me where you were, or you get out of my bed right now. I was so fucking scared that I'd lost you. I threw up twice this morning because I was so nervous. Three times yesterday."

His playful expression turned serious. "Are you kidding?"

"Nope."

"I didn't mean to worry you."

"Well you did, so get on with it already. What happened?"

He tried moving closer but I countered his every move. I wanted him to know that I meant business; there'd be no cuddling until he fessed up.

He said, "When I left your house I headed south. It took me a while to find someone who was willing to pick me up. The streets were pretty empty with it being Christmas and all, and those who rolled by were judgmental assholes. It wasn't until around ten at night that this dude let me into his Volvo."

"Ten? Oh my God, Pat. Weren't you freezing?"

He nodded, sliding towards me again. This time I didn't counter his advances. I was lucky he hadn't frozen to death.

"I second guessed whether or not I should get in, but he reminded me a bit of you, and I was desperate to get out of the cold. We drove around just shootin' the breeze like guys do. He told me that he was headed to his house out west and asked whether I wanted to join him. I didn't have anything better to do and I'd never been out that direction, so I said OK. The house was pretty small even for a single dude, and deep in the woods. It didn't take long for me to realize why. He had a massive weed growing operation going on. Apparently he had only come our direction to make a deal with a couple of buyers. I stayed there a few days, sampling the plants and learning about the business. It was totally chill and I didn't want to leave. But I wanted to keep my promise to you, so I began my journey home...

"...He loaded me up with a sack of grass at no charge, and told me how to get more once I came back to school. I blew through it pretty fast. I guess I was just pissed that no one wanted to pick me up. Though, come to think of it, I probably reeked of weed and stale skin, and I hadn't shaved the entire time I was there. The only people who asked if I wanted a ride were fellow hippies going the opposite direction. I ended up walking all the way up until I could afford the bus fare here. I'm tired as shit and broke as shit, so please don't give me shit for the delay. I don't have the energy."

I didn't know where I had expected him to say he had been, but it certainly wasn't out west, playing house with a drug dealer. A part of me was jealous that he'd had such an interesting break while I sat at home with my 'rents. But mainly I was worried.

He had spent his break doing drugs, something that I never had the desire to touch because it seemed so stupid to. I knew that it was true that a lot of people were doing them. Some people even claimed that they could be beneficial. But it didn't sit well with me that he had gone on such a binge and that, now that I thought of it, he looked like he was high. Or maybe he wasn't high. Maybe he was just as tired as he said he was. I didn't know. I didn't have enough experience with drugs to tell the difference between someone who had recently taken a toke and someone who was just worn out.

Pat was patient with me while I tried to think of a response. When several minutes passed in silence, he began massaging my back. I was tense, but he managed to get out all of my knots.

"You're not mad at me are you?" he asked.

I shrugged, still speechless. *Drugs.* I thought. *Pat is on drugs.*

"Is it that I was gone for so long? Look I already told you, I tried to get back on time. If I had known how long it would take me, I may not have gone so far."

"So you're into drugs now?" I asked bluntly.

He pulled away from me, appearing hurt. "If by into 'them' you mean I like weed then yeah, I guess you can say that. That's all I've tried so far. I promise it's nothing to worry about. It just takes the edge off, you know?"

"The edge off of what?"

He pulled my hair away from my neck and kissed it softly. My body shivered in response so he continued, kissing me between each word that he spoke. "School," Kiss. "Clones," Kiss. "Life," Kiss. "And everything else."

"That's funny," I said. "You never needed help with that before."

"Before what?" his expression grew dark.

"Before the night of the party," I said, getting up from the bed. "You've changed since then, and you won't tell me what happened. I'm concerned about you. You're not you anymore."

He cracked his knuckles, one at a time. "I don't want to talk about it," he said.

"I know you don't, but you have to."

"Do I?" he asked.

I hated the way his voice sounded, like guitar strings that had been wound too tight. I decided to back down. I didn't want to do anything to push him away after he had had been gone for so long. I didn't want him to fade.

"Forget I mentioned it," I said.

I arranged a pile of dirty laundry on the floor to form some sort of a mattress. I wasn't about to sleep on my ex-roommate's bed without sheets. The mattress was stained yellow from age and, for reasons unknown, smelled like cat piss.

"What's that for?" Pat asked.

"To sleep on. You keep the bed, I'm good down here."

Pat sprang up, "Oh no, I can't let you do that. You take the bed." Examining the size of it he added, "Or we can try sleeping together. We've got skinny asses."

I lay down and turned away from him. "Just go to sleep already. You look awful, and our first class is at seven. Hodge won't be amused by your extended absence."

"Fine," he said, yawning. "Thank you, and goodnight June."

"You're welcome and goodnight Pat."

I didn't sleep at all, even though I was surprisingly comfortable. I couldn't stop thinking about Pat and how he was now doing drugs. It wasn't like he was shooting heroin or snorting cocaine. From what I heard, weed wasn't anything truly addictive. Still, I couldn't understand why he felt the need to do it in the first place. Was his life really so bad? Wasn't I making him happy?

I prayed that this was just a phase and that by next week he'd be clean. I didn't know what I'd do if he became a stoner, a stereotype that we had often fought against. But I was pretty sure that stoners didn't make good boyfriends.

Chapter 14: January 24, 1969

On a Friday after class ended Pat suggested we check out The Comet. The Comet was a restaurant just outside of town that was known for its live bands and the crowd of misfits it drew. I had never been there before and didn't even know it existed until Pat told me about it. It was a hole in the wall, and a hell of a hike to get there. But it sounded like something interesting to do.

Pat had frequented The Comet in high school, and had played a slew of gigs there. They paid him in beer, oblivious to the fact that he was way underage. He developed a bit of a following, mainly older girls who thought he was cute. I didn't bother asking whether he had gone out with any of them. I wasn't stupid. He was a handsome young guy with a belly full of beer, surrounded by women. Of course he did.

He performed there all the way up until he was about to graduate high school. One night after a particularly good set, the owner asked him if he'd like a more permanent arrangement. He could sing there every weekend, for an hour or two, earning a percentage of the waitress's tips. Best of all, he could still have all of the beer he could keep down. Pat considered the offer, but didn't go through with it. He never played at The Comet again.

I asked him why he rejected such a sweet gig and he shrugged.

"The owner was a real nice guy, but there was freedom in turning him down. I didn't want playing there to turn into anything serious. When he made me that offer, I knew that's what was happening."

"I bet the girls were disappointed you left," I said.

"I'm sure they got over it," he said flatly.

The restaurant was dimly lit with paper lanterns and orange lava lamps. There was a long bar to the right, and several tables filled with young people smoking cigarettes and grass. The stage was all the way in the back, occupied by two chicks with legs for days and plump lips painted pink. One was playing guitar while the other sang. Her voice was raspy and a thousand times better than anything on the radio.

We snagged the table closest to the stage and Pat lit a joint.

"Really?" I asked, glaring at him. "We're out having a good time. There's nothing to be stressed about."

He waved me away, "It's fine June. Let's just listen to the music."

"Can't you have fun with me without putting shit into your body? Am I that boring?"

"You're the last thing from boring."

"Then why do you need a joint?"

"I just do okay?"

I shook my head. "No. Actually, it's not okay."

He threw his hands into the air. "This has nothing to do with you. Just let it go already."

"Fine," I seethed. "But I want you to know that it has *everything* to do with me."

I fled to the bathroom to get away from him. I splashed my face with lukewarm water before applying a fresh coat of cherry lip balm. I still wasn't ready to go back and face Pat, so I went into a stall and read the graffiti. Written with lipstick and black markers were things like "Eddy + Marge Forever" and "Love is everything." There was even a crude drawing of two stick figures having sex.

The more I read, the shittier I felt about snapping at Pat. He had asked me to back down, and I'd refused. I wasn't even sure why I had gotten so angry, or why he had risen to the occasion. Was I the worst girlfriend ever for storming off like that? Or had he earned it?

When I returned to our table, I watched the women up on stage, so good looking and so confident. Pat had stubbed out the joint while I was gone, replacing it with a bottle of Coke. I scooted close to him, letting him know that I was sorry. He wrapped an arm around my shoulder, and I guessed that he was sorry too.

The band finished a slower song, and then took a quick break. When they came back they were joined by a third girl with a tambourine. She shook it energetically, transforming their sound from chill to upbeat in a matter of seconds. I suddenly had the urge to dance, and pulled Pat out of his seat.

"What're you doing?" he asked.

I dragged him to the side of the room which was unoccupied by people and furniture. "Come on, let's dance," I said, swaying my hips back and forth fluidly. I stretched my arms into the sky and swayed them too. I got lost in the beat, experiencing a sense of flow similar to when I was painting. It wasn't until a few songs in that I noticed Pat hadn't joined me. He was standing cross armed and stiff as a board.

"What's the matter?" I asked.

"You look really sexy," he said. His pupils were the size of quarters, and he tugged at the inner seam of his jeans.

"Don't sound so surprised," I teased.

He laughed. "I'm not surprised. I've always known you were beautiful, but tonight I can't stop looking at you. God I'm lucky."

"Take a picture, it'll last longer," I winked.

"Way to be a cheeseball," he said.

He ran his hands down my waist and over my butt. I ran mine through his messy hair, and pulled him closer. I could feel his heart beating against my chest, and that he was hard. His breath came out in ragged bursts as I slid my hands under his shirt and over his groin. He grinned wickedly.

"Get a room," someone shouted.

Shit. I had forgotten we were in a restaurant, surrounded by people.

I turned to see who had shouted as a man with wiry arms approached us. He looked sort of like Pat but with red hair slicked back into a ponytail and a beard. He smelled like tea tree oil and coconut.

"Hey dude," Pat shook the guy's hand then pulled him in for a hug. "How've you been?"

"Been pretty busy," the guy said. "Who's the stone fox you're dancing with?"

Pat introduced us. "This is my girlfriend, June," he said. "June, this is Dag. He owns the place. He's the one I was telling you about, the guy who set me up with gigs a while back."

"It wasn't so long ago," Dag said. "And the offer still stands."

Pat pulled out a cigarette and lit it. "Nah, I've taken a break from performing."

"That's such a shame. You know, I think you could've made it big if you tried," Dag said. "You shouldn't waste your talent."

I laughed. "That's exactly what I said to him. The worst part is that he doesn't play at all anymore."

"See? You should always listen to your gal. I learned that the hard way." Dag pointed to his wedding ring.

"Shit, you're married now? Congrats dude. How'd that happen?"

Dag twisted the ring off his finger and passed it to Pat. He held it up to his eye like a spy glass, reading the inscription: "Forever and always."

Dag answered, "I met a girl unlike any other, and I did what I had to do to keep her." He rubbed his beard. "She threatened to leave if I didn't pop the question. I thought she was kidding; I didn't know she was the marrying kind. But then one day, she tried breaking up with me. I proposed right then and there. Marriage suits us, even more than either of us thought it would. My only regret is not asking sooner."

Pat passed the ring back to him and said jokingly, "I don't remember receiving a wedding invitation." He pretended to whimper. "I thought we were closer than this."

Dag rubbed Pat's shoulders in fake consolation. "Hey, cheer up brother. My own mother wasn't invited to the shindig. We kept it real quiet. We didn't want to make a big fuss."

"That's cool. All that matters is that you did it," Pat said. "The other stuff is just frill."

"Exactly."

Pat wrapped his arm around my waist and kissed my neck, letting me know he hadn't forgotten me. "Well, I'm happy for you man. I really am," he said, "and the band tonight was great. But if you don't mind, I think we're going to head out." He pulled me closer, and I leaned my head against his shoulder.

"Are you sure? If you stay I can hook you up with some beer like old times. No charge," Dag said.

"Yeah, I'm sure. I think June and I want to go somewhere a little more private."

Dag nodded. "Right on. Well it was nice meeting you, June. Keep this guy out of trouble, and don't forget the rubber."

I pretended to laugh at his joke. "We won't."

Pat finished his cigarette before setting it in an ashtray.

I whispered in his ear, "Race you to my dorm? I still don't have a roommate you know."

He broke into a sprint and I struggled to keep up with him. We made it back in record time.

Chapter 15: February 21st, 1969

The bleachers of the gymnasium were barely visible beneath the horde of basketball fans waving their navy blue paraphernalia. They roared at one another so loudly that at first I thought I had arrived late to the game. When I noticed that the only people on the court were slim women in pleated skirts waving pom-poms and doing splits, I knew that I was on time. I told several scowling classmates to "scooch" and sat at the end of the first row. The seats were even harder than I had imagined, offering zero back support for those of us who lacked even a basic level of core strength.

Where the frig is Pat? I wondered, consulting the scoreboard to our left. *The game's going to start any minute now.*

He had insisted that I go to this game with him despite how much I hated sports. I wasn't even sure why he wanted to go so badly. He had never shown any interest in basketball, and was leery of all athletes. When I told him that if he really wanted to go to the game, he could go by himself, he looked so hurt that I changed my tune. If attending this game was really that important to him, I'd do it. I'd have done anything to make him forget about taking a toke for five minutes. Hell, I would've even gone to church if that's what he wanted.

Pat always seemed to be smoking these days. Cigarettes, joints, cigars; it didn't matter. The only time he wasn't surrounded by a cloud of smoke was the few times he showed up for class. Even then he sat clicking his lighter on and off beneath his desk so loudly that he was often dismissed. I'd spend the remainder of class watching him pace back and forth outside, wafts of whatever he was nursing that day sneaking in through the cracks of the ill-insulated window.

Afterwards I'd lecture him for leaving me alone with the clones only to contract lung cancer, or I'd tell him that he was wrecking his voice. I hadn't heard him sing in months, but I wanted him to be able to if he ever picked up the hobby again. Pat never failed to change the subject or to laugh off my concerns, and I'd let him.

The commotion of the crowd standing in unison shooed away my thoughts about Pat. The basketball team was lined up behind the doors diagonal from the crowd, ready to make the same ridiculous entrance they probably did every home game. I could see through the window that Jesse was at the front. His gaze wasn't focused on the rowdy crowd or the basketball hoops. It was on the asses of the two cheerleaders in the center of the court, prepared to unroll a flimsy white banner when cued.

"Ladies and gentlemen," an upperclassman with an impressive mustache boomed, "Please welcome…. the *Wravington Ravens!*"

The crowd stomped their feet and applauded as the team bolted onto the court. The team stood at the sides of the banner that had just been unfurled while the cheerleaders began their opening chant.

"Ravens, Ravens. Here they come! Ravens are, number—"

Their cheering came to a sudden halt when one of the coaches rushed onto the court, pointing at the banner. The word "Raven" had been painted over with thick black paint so that it now read, "Go Wravington Rapists!"

The girls holding the banner looked at one another, no doubt wondering if they should tear the thing up. The basketball team shifted from side to side, studying their over-sized feet. After several seconds of silence so painful that only the devil himself could have orchestrated it, the audience became an audio collage of giggles, shouting, and knee slapping. The banner was swiftly escorted off of the court, but that didn't stop the laughter. People were amused by what they had perceived as a prank, probably aimed at horrifying the school's deans. I was the only one who saw it for what it was: a protest. But who was crazy enough to attempt such a stunt? And why?

I was looking around at the animals that surrounded me when the one person who was not laughing caught my eye. Pat stood by the gymnasium entrance with his brows drawn together and jaw quivering. He exited through the wide-barred doors that slammed behind him, a cigarette already in hand.

I followed him out of the gym and struggled to keep up with his swift pace. I didn't say anything to him at first, too frightened by the glazed look in his eye and the fact that he kept repeating to himself, "They don't care. No one cares."

He made one loop around the building and then another. I thought about calling the cops, worried that he might be a danger to himself or someone else, but I shook the thought away. Pat wasn't a violent guy. Besides, the cops would be more likely to arrest him than to stage a psychological intervention.

By the third lap he stopped mumbling, and became noticeably calmer. We reached the parking lot and he leaned against a shiny gold Cadillac to light another cigarette. He had abandoned his first halfway through his first lap, or more accurately, chucked it at the side of the building like it was a dunk tank.

"Are you feeling better?" I asked, pressing the back of my hand against his forehead. It felt like a sponge that had been soaking in a bucket.

He winced. "Yeah" he said, "I'm fine."

I looked down at his fingers which were stained black.

"Why did you paint over that sign?" I asked.

Pat slid his hands into his pockets. "Oh, you know. I just wanted to see if I'd get away with it."

I rolled my eyes at his obvious lie then looked at him more thoroughly than I had in months. He was even lankier than when we met, just a bundle of bones wrapped in a thin layer of flesh. His hair was caked with grease, and his cheeks were dotted with tiny pink pimples. He was still the most handsome guy I had ever met, but I had to admit, he was looking scraggly.

"Sooner or later we're going to have to talk about what happened," I said. "It's eating at you. I can tell."

"Nothing happened," he said.

"You and I both know that's not true," I pressed. "Ever since the party you've been different. I knew something happened when you came out looking the way you did, but you never said anything so I let it drop."

"June, please."

"Then today, you painted over that sign. I mean what's that all about? Who *does* that?" My tone was accusatory, but I quickly became ashamed. All of the puzzle pieces from the night of the party until now were coming together. The bruises. The unzipped pants. The subsequent outbursts, smoking, and drug use.

"Oh my God. Jesse and the other guys who were in the apartment…they didn't just beat you up, did they? Pat, did they rape you?"

"I don't want to talk about it," he said flatly.

"We *need* to. If you don't want to talk about it, then why the hell would you stage a protest?"

"I don't fucking know," he said. "I didn't think it through. I just did it okay?"

"Come on, there has to be a better reason than that. Tell me about what happened at the party. I promise I won't judge you for it."

"*Judge me* for it? For fucks sake!" He screamed. Then lowering his voice he said, "Can't you just leave me alone?"

"You can't keep shutting me out like this," I said. "You need help. I can help you."

He shook his head and mumbled under his breath. "Nobody can help me. Not even you."

"What?"

"I said…" he paused. "I said I'm getting hungry."

"That's not what you said."

"I thought you didn't hear me."

"Well, I guess I did."

We started walking again, making more laps around the gym. I only spoke once I sensed he wouldn't fly off the handle.

"Do you want to get a veggie burger or something?" I asked.

"Not really."

"How about some Chinese food?"

He shook his head.

"I know," I said. "Let's go to the store and buy every type of cookie they have. My treat."

He bowed his head. "I just want to go to my room and lie down," he said.

"Are you sure?" I asked.

Pat didn't respond. He just walked away without saying another word. I didn't bother following him.

Chapter 16: February 22nd, 1969

I hated the way I had acted after the basketball game. I felt like I was to blame for Pat leaving all flustered and without saying goodbye. How stupid was I to say that I wouldn't judge him for being raped? And why the hell did I think that cookies would resolve his problems? He wasn't a fucking toddler.

I waited until late afternoon to reach out to him, figuring he needed time to cool off. When I finally called over to his dorm asking to speak with him, I didn't expect him to come on the line. I wouldn't have answered if I were him.

"Hello?" Pat asked.

I leaned back in my chair. "Hey, it's me."

"Oh hey, June. What's up?"

I was taken aback by his cheerful tone. "I'm sorry about yesterday. I was a complete shithead."

"You could never be a shithead," he said seriously.

"Well, I sort of was. Want to get ice cream with me? I want to see you...I miss you."

"Miss me? You just saw me yesterday."

"Well I do."

The phone went silent for a minute, and I thought maybe he had hung up. Then in a mocking tone he asked, "You want to get ice cream in the middle of winter? Are you trying to ruin my figure?"

"You caught me," I said. "I plan on stuffing your face with chocolate sundaes until I'm the only one in this relationship with a bony ass. Is it a crime?"

"Damn straight it is. I happen to like my bony ass. You know, if I had my handcuffs on me, I'd place you under arrest for such a remark."

And with that the Pat I had fallen in love with was back.

"You don't own handcuffs," I said.

"You don't know that."

We walked into town slowly, despite the wind that made our coats feel like summer sheets. The streets were completely barren, probably owing to the freezing temperature.

The ice cream store was open six days a week, and never closed for inclement weather. Even in the event of an apocalypse I guessed that the owner would still be there, waiting on cockroaches. I loved this little store, and Pat did too. Its roof was red and white striped, like a circus tent draped over a take-out container. Its inside was stuffed with tiny pastel tables and mismatched chairs that looked like they belonged in a royal garden. We had become regular customers there, and whenever we went, we moved from table to table, deciding which color best fit our mood and switching chairs around until we achieved our childish visions.

Pat went to the back of the shop and selected a powder pink chair for himself, while I chose a blue one for me. We dragged them to a green table by the window and feigned discontent; the green and the pink were too reminiscent of a watermelon for a day like today. We dragged them over to a yellow table instead, and nodded to one another, satisfied.

He ordered his usual—double chocolate with malt and fudge topping —while I mixed it up with one scoop each of strawberry and chocolate. Even the owner was surprised that I had veered from a wet walnut sundae, and questioned whether he had heard me properly.

"Oh, she's feeling rebellious," Pat said. "After this we're going to rob the bank across the street. If you keep quiet, we'll give you a generous share."

The owner cracked a grin. "Wonderful. I expect to have my cut by five-thirty."

We returned to our table and indulged on the creamiest ice-cream known to man. The next people to enter the shop were an elderly couple whose voices trembled as they ordered one cone to share. They were several inches smaller than the average person, their bones having shrunk with age. The woman had a crooked back, and stark white hair that had been arranged into a neat bun. The man wore a fancy jacket with a shiny watch dangling out of his pocket.

"I want to be like them someday," Pat said as they were leaving.

"Decrepit and stingy?" I asked. I hadn't intended for it to come out so harshly, but there it was. Who orders one scoop for two people? They hadn't looked like they were hurting for money.

"No," Pat said. "Didn't you notice? They were holding hands the whole time. Even when they were paying they didn't want to break apart. I bet they're more in love than most newlyweds."

I contemplated this while he stuffed his napkin into his cup. It was stained brown from wiping a pound of fudge off of his face. Lord, he didn't know how to eat without making a mess.

"I think we can manage that," I said at last. "We're already happier than most couples are, wouldn't you agree?"

He nodded.

"Well, let's keep it going."

"Easy as that?"

"Easy as that."

We sat silently for a couple of minutes, just looking around and digesting. Another couple walked in and ordered two vanilla milkshakes to go. I wondered why so many people sought out ice cream in this horrible weather, and why so few people lingered in the warmth of the shop.

"You know what I just realized?" Pat asked.

"What?"

"We never did anything for Valentine's Day."

I shrugged, trying my best to appear unperturbed. When Valentine's Day came and went without a single flower or mention, I just figured we were "that" couple. You know, the couple that boycotts the holiday for being too commercial or cheesy or some other reason.

Had I wanted to celebrate? I'd be lying if I said no. I had spent my entire life single on Valentines Day, while my friends from cheerleading went out on dates with various yahoos. Of course I wanted to celebrate, but I wasn't going to let Pat in on that secret. I didn't want to seem needy.

"I'm so sorry," he said. "I only just realized it because of that heart over there," he pointed to a decal on the display case. "I should've taken you out or written you a letter or something."

"It's okay," I said. "I forgot about it too."

"Bullshit. You're pisspoor liar June. Your face gives everything away."

I shifted in my seat, almost tipping the table over.

"I'll tell you what. I'm going to make it up to you. On one of those rare nice days when Old Man Winter cuts us a break, we're going to have our own Valentine's Day. Does that sound like a plan?"

I agreed that this was a cool idea and asked him what we were going to do. He said it would be a surprise, and that I didn't have to worry about a thing; he'd arrange it all. We stayed for a while longer before throwing away our cups and saying goodbye to the owner.

"Five-thirty," he said pointing to his watch. "Don't forget my share."

"Never," Pat joked. "Hell, maybe we'll have it by four."

Chapter 17: May 9th, 1969

It wasn't until spring that we celebrated Valentines Day. For one thing, the weather hadn't exactly been on our side. We never did have one of those unseasonably warm days and Pat insisted that it had to be. For another, Pat had been placed on academic probation.

The school had finally gotten wind of the fact that he rarely attended class unless it was to take a test or submit a project. He faired surprisingly well for someone who didn't crack open a book or listen to lectures, earning A's much to the frustration of his professors. They didn't understand how someone who didn't put in an ounce of effort could flourish academically, especially when that person walked around high half of the time. My theory is that one of them turned him in out of jealousy. None of my professors ever struck me as being as intelligent as they pretended to be.

The college's backwards-ass policy to "punish" Pat was to suspend him for a period of three weeks while they came up with a plan of action. I guess they figured that if he wasn't going to attend class, they wanted it to be on their terms rather than his. The whole thing seemed like a power trip, but Pat did as he was told.

During his suspension, Pat wasn't allowed to leave his room, except to go to church or the bathroom. He also wasn't allowed visitors and was under the careful surveillance of the Head Resident, meaning that there was no way I could risk sneaking in.

Just so that we could see each other, he and I became regulars at church. Listening to the priest was worth it so long as we could hold hands in the back pew for an hour or two. At least, that's what we did on Pat's good days. Some days he was too high to stay awake, and would rest his head on my lap for a long nap. On these days I was embarrassed to be with him. As boring as the services were, I still thought that everyone should be respectful during them.

When services ended I'd shake him awake and give him the silent treatment. He'd apologize, looking truly disturbed for having checked out, but I still wouldn't talk to him.

After his suspension, they made a deal with him. If he became a model student and attended all classes from then until the end of the semester, they wouldn't automatically fail him for having missed so many lectures. If he missed even one, unless excused by a doctor's note, he would be kicked out of college. The same mandate applied to all rule-breaking. Even minor violations such as forgetting to bring a pencil to class became grounds for expulsion.

Pat signed a paper stating that he understood the consequences of his actions if they were to remain unchanged, making the whole thing official. From then on he was as good as his word, showing up exactly on time and not getting dismissed early. He still didn't interact with the professors like he had during first semester; he didn't ask questions and he never raised his hand. He spent most of his time writing song lyrics in his notebook and doodling. But at least he made an appearance.

As soon as class let out he would chain smoke and complain about how boring it all was, how he was wasting his time. I told him that I was proud of him for following the rules, and that everything would be worth it once we graduated. Despite his grumpiness, I knew he was secretly happy that they'd given him a chance to clean up his act.

By early May the weather had reached the mid seventies, so he and I had taken to lying on the hill by the gym. He talked his fair share about things ranging from inequality to war to how inappropriately shaped the lamps posts by the library were. I talked about finals and how much I was looking forward to getting them over with already.

On a Friday after classes let out, we were hanging out at our usual grassy hangout spot when Pat had an idea. "Today we're going to celebrate Valentine's Day," he said.

"We don't have to do that." I said, "We can just celebrate next year." I ripped up a clump of grass and let it fall through my fingers like confetti.

"Don't be such a downer. I have all sorts of ideas, and today's the perfect day for them."

I sighed. "Alright, but I don't have a present to give you or anything."

"Who said that I want one? Today's all about you."

I listened as he instructed me to go back to my dorm for a couple of hours while he got things ready, and then watched as he practically skipped towards town.

When I got back to my dorm I tried all sorts of things to pass the time. Reading, sleeping, drawing, singing, but nothing could distract me from wondering where we'd be going. There were only so many things to do in our small town, and he and I had just about done them all. What was there to be excited about?

He showed up two hours later, tapping my window with a tree branch. I flipped him off to let him know I had seen him, and joined him out on the lawn. He kissed my hand as though he were my escort, and I his fair lady. I curtsied in return, and said in my most obnoxious British accent, "Where to, handsome sir?"

Several clones sniggered as they saw us, but we didn't care. If anything, their disapproval added to our joy.

"You'll see," he said, promenading me over to the road.

A VW bus was parked with its side door wide open. It was yellow with dirty rims and a white peace sign painted on its rear window. The inside was outfitted with a shag rug that was muddy and torn, along with a fold-out table with rainbow placemats and a used ashtray.

A bus this psychedelic could only belong to Pat, but I had no idea where it had come from. Freshmen weren't allowed cars on campus, unless it was a temporary arrangement, and he hadn't mentioned anything about owning one before.

"You dig?" he asked as I poked around inside. "I bought it off of Dag yesterday. It was a steal. He even agreed to let me park it at The Comet if I threw in an extra ten."

Other than the thick scent of weed that hung about the cabin, I certainly did dig it. By now I had joined Pat in smoking the stuff, but I still didn't like the smell. Weed had made a regular appearance in our Parker Hall cocoon, and eventually I could no longer contain my curiosity. I tried it and became a weekly user, not because I wanted to, but because it was there. At first I wondered why I didn't try it sooner. It really did take the edge off of things just like everyone said. But what nobody tells you is how boring it gets after the first couple of uses, giving birth to the urge to try something a little stronger. Neither one of us had given in to this urge yet, but that didn't mean that it wasn't there.

Pat's new ride was just the sort of thing that we needed to escape the confines of our campus, and it had an ample amount of space for the two of us to mess around. He slid the side door closed and opened the passenger for me. I climbed in, knocking over a bottle of wine that was perched in my seat. He mumbled something under his breath and stashed it in the trunk. Returning to the front of the car, he placed his keys in the ignition and we rolled out of the lot slowly, ignoring the groan of the engine as he switched gears.

We drove through the town and past the church where my mom was probably playing bridge or cleaning the pews. We drove past my old high school and the field where cheerleading practice had been held every Monday through Thursday in the fall. We drove past everything and everywhere I had ever known, and it was then that I realized how small my world had been before meeting Pat. Now that we were together and had a set of wheels to call our own, nothing seemed off limits.

After a couple of hours he pulled into a parking lot that was almost empty. I had no idea where we were. By the number of trees I thought we were at some sort of a park or maybe a campground. I ripped open my door eager to find out, but Pat reached across me and shut it.

"Oh no you don't," he said. He popped open the glove compartment which was stuffed with cigarettes, Red Hots, and a bandana. He handed me the latter and told me to blindfold myself.

"You're kidding me," I said. "No way."

"Please? It's all a part of the experience."

"Only if you insist."

"I really do."

I covered my eyes with the scratchy material and tied it tightly.

Pat slammed his door behind him and then opened the trunk. I heard him rummaging around it, then another slam. He opened my door for me and helped me out of the bus, made more difficult by the fact that he only used one hand. I guessed that the other hand was carrying something, like maybe the wine he had hidden earlier.

At the beginning of our journey, the ground was smooth and easy to navigate. I asked him whether we were almost there and he grunted, saying that we had further to go. As time wore on the terrain became uneven, and I struggled not to trip over tree roots and rocks and other dangers that I couldn't see. Pat held me steady, even as we began our trek uphill and the sun beat heavily down on us. His breathing became heavier, his lungs gasping for oxygen to make up for his exertion. The journey from campus to wherever we were marked the longest he had gone without smoking in months. I wondered if his body could even process such clean air.

Just when it seemed like we would be walking for all eternity, we stopped. He took his time positioning me towards whatever he wanted me to see and said, "Keep your eyes closed, okay?"

I nodded. He removed the blindfold then laced his fingers through mine.

"You can open them now."

Ahead of us was a canyon of emerald foliage splashed against a clear summer sky. It was vast and never ending, as though infinity itself was stretched before us, dazzling us with its divine splendor. It was one of those sights that humbles any onlooker, reminding us how large the world is and how insignificant we are in comparison.

I didn't know what to say in response to such a view. Nothing seemed appropriate. So instead I turn around and kissed Pat with enough passion to match the beauty that surrounded us. He matched my passion tenfold, and I allowed him to lead. We stood there making out, and then rolled onto the ground, getting really into it.

When Pat finally released me, I noticed what he had been toting with him up the canyon: a wicker basket containing lunch, wine, and a blanket. He spread the blanket out on the grass overlooking the most extraordinary view I had ever seen, and then asked if I was hungry. I nodded while he uncorked the wine and passed it to me. I took a sip and tried not to cough as the bitter liquid slid down my parched throat and into my empty stomach.

"Sorry it's not the best," he said, noticing my sour face. "I stole it from an upperclassman. I guess he has shitty taste."

He took the bottle from me and tried it for himself. Spitting it out he added, "*Really* shitty taste."

I unpacked the lunch containers and plastic utensils. There was cucumber potato salad, stuffed celery, cheese sandwiches, and a package of cookies. We ate a majority of the food then ripped up what was left and sprinkled it onto the grass. It seemed like a waste to throw it away when we were in the wilderness. Even if the only thing that ate it was ants, it would be well worth our trouble. We guessed that before then it would be picked up by the bird that had been eyeing us from the tree behind us, nervously pacing from side to side on a branch.

We gaped at the canyon for a while after that, still amazed by its natural grandeur. At one point I observed Pat who appeared pensive yet at peace, almost like when he was sleeping. There wasn't a feature on his body that hadn't been perfectly placed, not a part of his soul that needed changing. There was no doubt in my mind that I truly loved this man, and the timing finally felt right to tell him.

"What?" he asked, growing aware of my gaze.

I really had been staring a long time. If I had been anyone else, he would have found it creepy.

"Nothing," I said, "it's just that I...um..."

Oh God. Was it really so hard to say? I love you, I love you, I love you. Yes, I knew how the phrase should go, even if I had never said it to anyone but my relatives. But what if his answer wasn't what I wanted to hear? What if, after all this time, he wished we had remained just friends?

"I love you," I said finally. "Like, a lot."

Pat smiled his crooked smile and I knew everything was going to be okay. "June, I've loved you since the day we met. I'm glad you caught up with me."

"Really?" I asked. "That long ago?"

He nodded and exhaled completely. I wondered if some part of him had been holding his breath since day one.

"I love you," he said. "I loved you then, and I love you now. I'll always love you."

"Me too," I said, relieved. "I promise."

Chapter 18: August 15th, 1969

"What're you doing this weekend?" Pat asked.

I twirled the phone cord around my finger and leaned against the kitchen counter. The cool luster-rock sent shivers from the base of my spine up to my neck. I tugged my crop-top down, but it was too short to cover the chilled skin.

"Nothing much. My parents are away," I said, thinking that if they *had* been home I would've worn something much less revealing.

"Cool beans," Pat said. "So you're coming to Woodstock with me, right?"

"Woodstock?"

"Yeah, that big festival of love I was telling you about. You know, the one where Bob Dylan might make an appearance."

I unraveled the knot I had created then stretched the phone to the table. I used my shoulder to prop the phone against my ear while I grabbed a banana from the fruit bowl. Peeling back its speckled skin I said, "You know he's not actually going to show up right?" I bit into it and gagged. It was mushy and overly sweet, like baby food.

"He might. If I were him I'd totally perform at it."

I chucked the rest of the banana into the trash bin and went over to the sink. Filling a glass with water I said, "Oh you would, would you?"

"Hell yes I would. Performing outside to a crowd full of people just like us? What more could a guy want?"

"I just think the whole thing sounds too good to be true," I said taking a sip of my drink.

"Don't be so negative," he said. "It's going to be fun. I'm going with or without you, but I'd rather have you to enjoy it with."

"Will we be home before Sunday dinner?" I asked. "If I'm not back before my parents, they'll flip."

"Is the Pope Catholic? Of course I'll have you back by then, if that's what it takes to get you to go. We might miss a few acts on the back half of the show, but I'm ok with that."

I rolled my eyes. "Fine."

"Fine as in you're coming?"

"Yep. You're right; it could be fun. If not it's at least something to do."

"That's the spirit. I'll pick you up in a few."

"Catch you on the flip side."

As I waited for Pat, I packed a fringed hobo bag with some fruit and a change of clothes. Given that the festival was only three days long, I figured I wouldn't need much. I could always buy food when I got there. I looked at myself in the mirror and decided that the outfit I had on would do. It was sexy enough that Pat would have a hard time taking his eyes off of me, but it didn't beg for attention. My hair was a different story. I counted on my fingers how many days it had been since I brushed it. It had been four. As I navigated its knots and pulled out a chunk the size of a mouse, I was grateful that I had at least washed it.

I looked out of my window just as Pat was rolling up in his VW. He got out and grabbed a bouquet of fresh daisies off of the passenger's seat.

I ran out to greet him. "What's all this?" I asked, taking the flowers from him with one arm and hugging him with the other.

His gaze shifted to my bare stomach and his pupils became the size of dinner plates. "I passed a meadow on the way here and stopped to pick some. You like these right?"

"They're my favorite." I kissed him on his cheek, and my lips tingled from his stubble.

He softly nibbled my lips then trailed down to my stomach to kiss my belly button. I could tell he was dying to do more than this but my neighbor, Ms. Nelle, had stopped gardening. She popped her head over her bushes, staring blatantly at the two of us. If her mouth had been open any wider, we could've shoved a whole beehive in it. We waved at her, and she scurried inside muttering something about kids these days.

When she was gone I climbed into the passenger side of the van. We drove for several hours, singing along to the radio when the signal was good, and making up our own tunes when it wasn't. I had a hard time imagining what this shindig was going to be like, and a part of me was nervous. I had never been to a real concert before, unless you counted the performances I saw down at The Comet. If Woodstock lived up to Pat's high expectations, it would be more special than all of these performances combined.

When we finally reached the farm where Woodstock was taking place, we ditched the van on the side of the road and headed into the festival. Thousands of people cluttered the area, overwhelming the concession stands and making it impossible to get near the stage. Pat and I walked arm in arm as we navigated through the crowd, searching for somewhere to sit where there weren't already people.

We settled on a patch of dirt next to a couple who were bare-assed and making love. At first I wanted to see whether Pat minded if we kept walking. The woman's moans were kind of distracting and I felt like we were invading their privacy. But I was getting pretty tired, and Pat didn't seem bothered by the couple.

Actually, I think he found them sort of cool. Not in a perverted sort of way, but in a semi-rebellious, semi-romantic one. I hoped that he wasn't getting any ideas.

The music began after the finale of their second go-round, but was soon interrupted when the great buckets in the sky tipped over. The farm went from dryer than a sack of breadcrumbs to hot fudge in a matter of minutes as people dashed in search of cover. Pat and I decided not to leave the spot that had taken us so long to procure. Our shirts clung to our bodies like cellophane and our jeans became soaked with brown liquid. Some people embraced the wicked weather by shedding their clothing and rolling around in the mud, while other people chanted "Let the rain stop!" as though Mother Nature would give a damn.

When the downpour finally let up and the music resumed, we felt like babies that had been forced to sit in our own filth. I stood to get something to eat from one of the stands, followed closely behind by Pat. I only made it a few feet because I couldn't stand the sloshing sound that my pants made as I walked, or the way that the drowned crotch hugged my lady-bits.

"Fuck this," I said, unbuttoning my jeans. I slid them down my thighs and kicked them off once they reached my ankles.

"You're joshin' me," Pat said, his mouth a perfect "O."

I removed my top and my undergarments then threw everything into a puddle.

"Well I'm not going to sit around like a wet sponge all night," I said.

I resisted the urge to cover myself while he eyed me up and down. Even though we had been going steady for months now, he had never seen me in the buff in broad daylight. Usually we messed around at night while most people were out partying or sleeping. Even then, it wasn't like we had been intimate that often. Sometimes when we were messing around, Pat would suddenly stop like he was no longer attracted to me or something. I'd get real self conscious thinking I had done something wrong, and he'd either suggest something else to do or leave.

Eventually Pat followed my lead, first peeling off his shirt then unbuttoning his drenched jeans. I tried not to look like too much of a weirdo as I watched him undress, but I also didn't want to look away. His body was pale and lean, as though he had never worked out a day in his life. For all the hair on his head, there was not a stitch of it on his body, except for on his legs. He was, by most girls' standards, unattractive, maybe even feminine. But I thought he was handsome.

When we were both fully nude, we walked to one of the concession stands. We waited for almost an hour in what we thought was a line, but was actually an angry mob. It turned out that everyone was angry because there was no food. The vendors had already sold out of everything, having severely underestimated the number of festival goers. No one knew if they were getting another shipment of supplies soon, or if that was it for the three days. Rumors began to circulate that some people were planning on burning the stands down.

Neither of us wanted to stick around to see if that happened. We pushed our way out of the crowd, and then split one of the oranges I had brought from home. We walked around savoring each juicy slice, our eyes pleading for someone to offer something better to eat. After finishing my share, I found myself craving the banana I had rejected earlier. At least it would've helped fill the void in my stomach.

"I'll be right back," Pat said once he had finished eating. "I'm going to go see if I can get us some real food from over there." He pointed to a huddle of people eating sandwiches across the way. Other than the fact that they weren't vegetarian (thick slices of ham were wedged between cheese and curly lettuce), the opportunity looked promising. There were several signs staked in the mud next to the group that read "Free Spirits Welcome."

As I watched him walk away from me, a cold hand pressed against the small of my back.

"Hey there, foxy momma."

The hand belonged to a guy with braided hair and flared pants. His breath reeked of alcohol and hemp.

"Come join us for some beer," he breathed.

I looked past him at his pals who were gathered around a cooler overflowing with bottles and ice. Judging by the blue cloud of smoke hovering above them, they were stoned.

"No, thanks," I said.

"You sure?" he wrapped his arm around my waist while I stared at him in disbelief. "We've got plenty. I'll even give one to your friend when he gets back."

I opened my mouth to protest, but I was pulled backwards with such force that I slid on a patch of mud. Pat caught me before I fell. His eyes lingered on mine as he asked if I was okay. I said that I was, and the man who had offered me beer moved closer.

"Fuck off," Pat barked at him.

"Chill out man. I was only trying to spread the good vibes."

"Get the hell away from her," Pat spat, lunging towards the man. Dodging the blow, the man backed away from us with his hands held up. Pat lunged at him again, but I caught his wrists.

"Cool it, Pat," I said, "What's the matter with you?"

His pulse was beating rapidly and beads of cold sweat gathered at his temples. He attempted to break free of my grip but fell. His knees sank deep into the mud as his nude body crumpled forward. The men with the beer pointed and laughed.

"Oh, Pat." I sank down alongside him and cradled his head against my bony chest. "Talk to me. Tell me what's going on."

Tendrils of his hair drained as he pressed closer to me. His head quivered like a bell that had been rung too hard. People gathered around us to watch what was going on. No one knew what they could do to help. I wished they would just go away already.

"C-can you take me home?" he stuttered.

His tears flowed down my breasts and into my navel where they formed a small pool.

"Yeah," I said, helping him to his feet. I wrapped his arm around my neck and guided him through the mob of muddied people, like a soldier that had been wounded in war. They stared at us as they ducked out of our way, but offered us everything from shelter to clothing to a ride home. The only things we accepted were cigarettes and a pack of matches. We lit one and passed it back and forth as we walked, watching the smoke rise into the air to suffocate the night sky.

"Do you want to tell me why you flipped out?" I asked, flicking ashes onto the ground. It was the first cigarette that I'd had in months, but I wasn't enjoying it. I was too upset by Pat's latest episode. Up ahead was the VW, barely visible amongst dozens of other vehicles haphazardly parked alongside the road.

Pat shrugged his shoulders, staring down at several pink scars on his wrists. They looked like they had been made with either a razor-blade or a pocket knife. When the first one had appeared at the beginning of summer, I made him promise never to hurt himself again. By the looks of it, he had broken that promise more than once.

"That guy could've taken advantage of you," he said after a long pause. "You need to be more careful."

"He wouldn't have done that," I said. "Not with that many people watching."

"Rape has nothing to do with intimacy. It's all about power and making someone feel worthless. That guy may have even enjoyed a good crowd. People are animals, June, fucking animals. You have no idea what they're like."

Pat's face bore the same haunted expression that he had worn the day of the basketball game and in his bedroom on Christmas morning. I had grown to fear this expression as much as I hated it. I was tired of seeing him unravel like this when he refused to talk about his pain. I knew that this was wrong of me, and I felt incredibly guilty for it. How could I, who hadn't been raped, be so frustrated with him?

The truth was it hurt being a bystander to his trauma. I felt like a passenger amidst turbulence, whose captain was staring blankly at the control panel. I wondered whether it was suicide to stay on this plane which seemed destined to crash, or whether I should parachute out of it while I still had the chance.

"Pat I think maybe we should take a break," the words tumbled out before I had a chance to process what I had said.

"You don't mean that," he said. "You promised you'd always love me, you can't just leave. Please don't." He placed his head in his hands and cried, even harder than he had earlier. He crouched down onto the road, unable to stand any longer.

I couldn't handle seeing him so broken, especially not when he was right. I hadn't truly meant what I said. I didn't actually want to split up. I was just out of things to say that I hadn't said before, and had allowed my hurt to do the talking.

Pat's chest heaved up and down rapidly, as though he were beginning to panic.

The muscles in my throat swelled. "You need to get better," I croaked. "For us. Talk to me, talk to somebody. I don't care. Just do something because I don't want to leave you."

He continued to sob, so I crouched down beside him.

"It's really hard seeing you like this," I said. "Don't you realize how much you're hurting me?"

He nodded, and took a moment to collect himself. "I'll try to get better," he said, standing up. "I swear to God that I will. I can't lose you, but I don't want to hurt you. I never meant to hurt you, you know that right?"

"I know," I said sincerely.

His lips were still quivering as he asked, "Can we go home now? As a couple?"

"As a couple," I repeated.

I handed him the cigarette and rummaged through my bag for the car keys. When I finally found them, Pat took them from me and insisted on driving. Silently we slipped into our spare clothing before heading back to his house for the rest of the weekend. Neither one of us mentioned Woodstock ever again.

Chapter 19: August 22nd, 1969

The last week of summer passed uneventfully. Pat and I didn't see each other because my parents kept me busy with chores and neighborhood functions, but we spoke on the phone every day. We talked about the upcoming year and the things we were looking forward to doing. We also talked about our majors and the fact that I was switching to art. Pat was proud of my decision to pursue something I was passionate about, even though it meant we'd be in separate classes. My mom, on the other hand, was appalled. She threatened not to pay tuition, but my dad cut in.

"I think art is an admirable major," he said. "It'll certainly teach June a thing or two about patience." He winked at me when my mom wasn't looking. He knew I had already made my decision. Telling them was merely a courtesy.

My mom contemplated it and then sighed, "I guess art is a more suitable major for a woman than history ever was. It may even help her develop an eye for good home design."

I cringed at her sexism, but let it go. It wasn't worth arguing over.

When Pat and I weren't discussing school, he talked about the various drugs that he wanted to try. He still hadn't done anything stronger than weed, but he wanted to. He was bored with the stuff, same as I was, and felt like it was no longer cutting it. I changed the subject each and every day until eventually he said he had scored LSD off of a regular at The Comet.

"I don't think LSD it is a good idea," I said seriously.

"Oh come on, June. Tons of people do it. I hear it's a real rush, real mind opening."

"Since when do you care what other people do?" I asked. "That shit can really mess you up. I thought you were trying to get better."

He hesitated and the phone crackled. I hoped we weren't about to lose connection, and that no one had hopped on the party line. Ms. Nelle from next door had been known to eavesdrop.

"You don't know that. It really helps some people. I feel like I have to at least give it a try," he paused. "I don't expect you to understand that. I'll let you know how it goes..."

"—Wait." I interrupted. "How much of it did you buy?"

"I don't know," he said. "A bunch."

It was my turn to pause. I had a sudden idea, and wanted to think it through. My gut told me it was a bad one, but I didn't know what else to do. I felt like I had two options. Break up with him for doing yet another thing to stress me out, or keep a closer eye on him.

"I'll do it with you when we get back to school," I said. "Just promise me that you'll wait until then."

"Seriously?"

"Uh-huh."

"Alright. Well if you're sure then I guess that would be ok. I can bring it to Parker Hall tomorrow. We can do it after we move in," he suggested.

"Perfect."

My mom shouted from the living room that it was time to go. Ms. Eleanor had invited us over to her house for brunch, and we were already late.

"I have to go," I told Pat. "See you tomorrow."

"See ya later alligator."

Ms. Eleanor lived across town, in a colonial mansion three times the size of our house. The only reason we ever visited was because my mom liked poking around the place, looking for ideas on how to improve our own home. Even though she found Ms. Eleanor's fashion sense disturbing, she felt she had a knack for interior design. They'd spend hours discussing everything from coffee tables to cornice, while I sat in the kitchen drinking freshly squeezed orange juice.

When we arrived a maid escorted us through the house and to the back porch. Several tables were set up with pitchers of lemonade, along with platters of fruit and cheese. There were children and some men, but mainly women in freshly starched dresses. My mom waved to some of them and whispered in my ear, "You don't think we're staying out here the whole time do you? We'll roast."

For once my mom was right. It was only midmorning, and already eighty degrees.

"I have no idea," I said. "But your face is beginning to melt. How much makeup did you put on anyway? It's a brunch not a strip joint."

My mom scowled at me. Several women from church called out to her, so she joined them at their table.

Before she could force me to say "hello," I grabbed a vine of grapes and walked around the backyard. The backyard was more modest than the house, containing only a flower garden and a small pond. I walked to the pond then swam my hands through the water, watching it ripple beneath my touch.

As I stood there I thought back to the conversation I'd had with Pat earlier. I couldn't believe that Pat had bought LSD, or that I'd agreed to do it with him. The Pat I'd met a year ago never would've touched that shit, and he wouldn't have brought me along for the ride. He'd changed so much since then, and many of these changes weren't good. I hated not knowing how many more changes were yet to come, or how they'd affect us.

"You've found my favorite thinking spot."

I turned to see Ms. Eleanor wearing a feathered hat and a skirt with roosters all over it.

"I'm not thinking," I said. "I'm just enjoying the view."

"Are you still with that boy I met at church on Christmas Eve?" she asked.

"I am," I said.

"Then it's just as I suspected. You're thinking about him." She came beside me and held onto my arm for support. The grass was still slick with morning dew, and we were on a bit of a slope. "He's troubling you," she said.

I shook my head. "Ms. Eleanor, shouldn't you go find some shade? It's really hot out here."

She laughed. "You can't get rid of me that easily. Tell me, what did he do to you?"

Sweat poured down my neck and back. I took a rubber band off of my wrist and pulled my hair into a low ponytail. "It isn't so much what he's done. It's what others have done to him."

She bobbed her head up and down. Her oversized hat slipped down over her forehead, nearly covering her eyes. "That's often the case," she said. "I've found that life is just one challenge after the next. Some are our own doing, but most aren't. In the thick of it all, we must remember that we always have choices. Do you understand?"

"I guess so," I said.

She took off her hat and began fanning herself with it. A fly buzzed by her ear.

"What do you do if someone you love makes the wrong choice?" I asked.

She placed her hat back onto her head. "We all make wrong choices," she said. "What matters is that we learn from them. Has he learned?"

I shrugged, "I don't really know yet."

"Then it's too early to tell."

Two ducks floated by. I was jealous of how peaceful they looked, and how simple their lives were compared to mine. "Are you saying that I should give him time to learn?" I asked.

"I'm saying that he has choices to make, and so do you."

She nodded back towards her house; most people had already gone inside to cool off. Only a few children remained on the patio, throwing chunks of cantaloupe at one another.

"Would you mind taking me inside? It's beastly out here. I can't remember the last time I sweat like this, but I think I was your age, and it involved a male."

I laughed. "Sure thing Ms. Eleanor. Whatever you want."

Back at the house, Ms. Eleanor's guests had begun brunch without her. They'd saved her a seat at the head of the table, but most of the food was already gone. I made up a plate with eggs and some toast then claimed my usual spot on a barstool in the kitchen. Servants bustled around me preparing dessert and asking me to taste test things here and there. When I wasn't sampling sparkling gelatin or pink Petit Fours, I was thinking about my choices, choices that would define my relationship with Pat, and ultimately my life.

Chapter 20: August 23rd, 1969

On move-in day I swiftly settled into my dorm. My new

roommate, Kyoko, had been anxiously awaiting my arrival. She

had already been there a week because she was an exchange

student and had to attend all sorts of special meetings. She spoke

English pretty well and seemed like someone I could get along

with. She asked whether she and I could get dinner together since

she didn't know anyone else, but I declined. I told her that my

boyfriend and I had already made plans but we'd be glad to hang

out with her another time. Her disappointment was made plain on

her face, but she said that she was looking forward to it and didn't

ask again.

Kyoko looked confused as I gathered my blanket and Christmas lights, but I pretended not to notice. I hadn't known her long enough to let her in on my Saturday night ritual, especially since this one would involve psychedelics. I hoped that by the end of the year, I would trust her enough to tell her about it. I thought it'd be nice to have a friend of the same gender. It would certainly make sneaking in and out of the dorm easier. Hell, maybe she'd even let Pat hang out in our room. My old roommate was never *that* cool.

I was the first to arrive at Parker Hall, even after several trips to the bathroom. My bowels were more nervous to try LSD than my mind was, and my bladder was out of control. I used just about every bathroom on campus on my way there, some of them more than once. I only hoped that a cloud of stink didn't follow me as I walked. I didn't want Pat to know what a mess I was.

When I finally got to the classroom, I tried focusing on the room's details to calm myself. The floor had been recently waxed and smelled slightly chemical. The blackboards had been washed and replenished with a fresh supply of erasers and chalk.

Am I really about to go through with this? I asked myself as I waited. Then I remembered Pat, and how much I loved him. *Yes, I have to, if only to keep him safe.* I lay down on my back, folding my hands over my stomach. I closed my eyes in an attempt to meditate.

Pat snuck into the room and straddled me.

I hoped that he couldn't smell my armpits as well as I could, so I laid into him as a distraction. He softly sucked my neck, gently massaging my breasts. I moaned. He knew my weak spots perfectly. I drew my head upward and traced my tongue over his lips. He wagged a finger playfully then pulled away.

"Are you ready to give it a go?" he asked.

"As ready as I'll ever be," I said.

He took the LSD out of his pocket. It looked like a stamp, right down to the image of the American flag.

"What do we do with it?" I asked as he handed me a tab of acid. I thought maybe we were supposed to stick it somewhere on our body like a Band-Aid.

"The guy I bought it from told me you just put it on your tongue and let it sit there until it dissolves," he said. "Are you ready?"

I took several deep breaths then nodded. My stomach gurgled loudly, and I willed it to calm down. Now was not the time to go running to the bathroom.

We counted down from three and stuck them into our mouths. The taste was neither citrusy nor bitter, the two flavors I had been expecting. It was bland like a stale communion wafer and I resisted the urge to spit it out. I wished that I had drunk some water ahead of time to help it along. I was pretty dehydrated from all of the shitting.

The effects of the drug weren't immediate, but I knew it was working when the logical part of my brain could no longer be reached. Thoughts entered two by two and, without a gatekeeper, burrowed in and out of my mind catalyzing both pleasure and chaos. I breathed as evenly as possible, trying to tame the dragon that had been unleashed in my consciousness. The classroom transformed into a kaleidoscope of shapes and colors that no language on this planet could convey. They mesmerized me, like a child seeing bubbles for the first time, and I lost all sense of who I was and where.

Eventually the drugs wore off. I don't remember how long it took. I came down off of the high pretty hard and fell asleep immediately afterward. It wasn't until I woke the next morning that I was with it enough to notice that Pat was gone. I remembered that during the trip, Pat had stood up and exited the room with a silver object in his hand. But that object had darted from wall to wall and I became dazzled by the trail of liquid diamonds it left in its path.

Now fully conscious, I worried where he might have gone and was pissed at myself for failing my mission. I was there to protect Pat, not to let him wander off without me. I ran out into the hallway screaming his name.

"Pat!" The shrillness of my voice was amplified by the emptiness of the corridor. "Pat!"

I turned a corner and saw the blurry outline of Pat's body surrounded by scarlet puddles.

His head tilted towards me as I approached, and he slid his pocket knife onto the floor. His arms were mutilated with rusty gashes overlapping one another, each competing to be the most gruesome. His abdomen was split open in several places beneath his ribs, and his hands were shaking.

I removed his shirt and balled up the fabric so that I could apply pressure to the freshest of the cuts. He winced but didn't cry out as the cotton absorbed the red goo.

"Why the hell did you do this?" I asked.

He put his hand on top of mine and attempted to sit upright. His calloused fingers traced small circles around my knuckles.

"LSD wasn't the cure that I thought it would be," he said at last.

I resisted the urge to say "I told you so," and kissed his damp forehead. "I'm glad you're ok," I said.

"Am I though?"

I checked on his wounds. A few were still bleeding, but most of them had clotted. It was likely that he would need stitches for some of the thicker slices, but he wouldn't die if he didn't receive immediate medical attention. The only way that he would die was if we ignored the wounds that don't bleed.

"It wasn't your fault," I said, massaging the crown of his head. "None of it was."

Pat shut his eyes and sighed heavily. His hair was sodden with grease but still beautiful. I had always been jealous of its effortlessness.

"You know that I'm here for you right?" I asked.

"You won't leave me?"

I shook my head. "Never. I'm sorry I made you think that I would. I didn't mean it. I was just hurting."

A hint of a smile flickered across his lips. He began singing so quietly that I had to lean in to hear it.

My daisy girl June, as strong as the sea,

My lover, my savior,

The best part of me.

A door opened somewhere near the front of the building. The gentle tapping of shoes against linoleum indicated that whoever had entered was heading straight towards us.

I looked at Pat with an expression that said "Should we split?" but he shook his head. There was no way that he'd be able to outrun anyone in his condition. All we could do was hold our breaths and hope for the best.

Professor Hodge walked by with his head buried deep in the Sunday paper. The headline said something about a war protest and he shook his head dismissively. "Idiots," he said, folding it up and sticking it into his back pocket. He passed where we were sitting and for a second we thought we were in the clear. But he paused at the end of the corridor and pivoted on his heels.

"You have two minutes to explain what happened here," he said, staring at Pat's blood. His skin became greenish and pale. "Then I believe a hospital visit is in order."

"Oh there's no need for that," Pat said, wincing as he tried to stand. One of his wounds peeled open, spilling fresh blood over his abdomen.

Professor Hodge looked like he was going to pass out. I wondered who needed medical attention more. "Two minutes," Hodge repeated. He peered at his watch. "I don't have all day."

I didn't know what to tell him. The truth? A lie? Which would result in the least amount of trouble? We liked Professor Hodge, and we were pretty sure that he liked us too. But Hodge was a man of discipline. He liked following the rules so long as they made sense, and doing drugs on campus certainly didn't make sense. There was no value to be gained from it, no bright future that could result. Just look at where we were now. Two hippies covered in blood, sweat, and tears. Literally.

Pat saved me from having to answer. "Honestly sir, it was an acid trip gone really, *really* wrong."

Hodge shook his head and whistled. "Yes, I'd say it certainly did. Were both of you involved in this nonsense?"

I opened my mouth to confess, but Pat swiftly shook his head. "No sir, just me. June and I were hanging out in the classroom over there—" he pointed in the direction of our groovy cocoon. "But she felt sick and left. I decided to stay behind and got bored. I thought that LSD would keep me entertained, but it resulted in this mess. She came looking for me this morning because we were supposed to get breakfast together and I didn't show. That's the only reason she's here."

I doubted that Professor Hodge believed him. My hair and makeup were a disaster from the night before, and my breath could kill. But for whatever reason, he decided to let these clues slide and said, "Well Pat, it has been a pleasure having you as a student, but I think it is safe to say that you'll be expelled. Let's get you to the hospital before those get infected, shall we?"

Pat hung his head. Despite how he sometimes acted, I knew that getting an education was important to him. What would happen once he got booted out of school? If he followed his parents' regime, he'd have to go into the military or try to enroll somewhere else. But what school would accept him after this?

We helped him to his feet and Hodge asked whether he needed an ambulance or could make it by car. Pat pleaded for the latter, so Hodge pulled his car around and told us not to get blood all over it. Pat and I rode in the back, while Hodge drove carefully through the morning church rush.

In the emergency room everyone looked at us like we were thieves. Women who had previously allowed their children free reign now beckoned them to sit down. Men who looked like they had been up vomiting all night stood defensively, with their arms crossed. I didn't know whether the stab wounds or the fact that we were hippies put them off more.

The woman behind the desk popped her gum and handed us a clipboard. She didn't look up from the papers as she told us to sign in. Pat took a pen from a shiny black cup then doubled over in pain. He swore so loudly that she gave him a once over. She punched several numbers onto her phone and muttered something into the receiver. Within minutes a nurse came out and escorted us into the back room.

Pat was in the ER for a couple of hours while they determined the severity of his injuries. Ultimately they decided that he looked worse off than he was. All they had to do was stitch him up and tell him to take it easy for a few days. They didn't ask too many questions which made things easier for us. We were too tired to think on our feet, and didn't want to end up in the psych ward.

The nurse wrapped Pat's abdomen with gauze and taped it. She helped him put on an olive green shirt, and I stifled a laugh. The shirt had come from the lost and found and was ten times too big for him. He reminded me of Dopey from *Snow White and the Seven Dwarves.* All he needed was a purple hat.

While they were giving Pat instructions on how to care for his wounds, Professor Hodge came back into the room. He had left almost immediately after we were taken back, claiming that he had a few things to take care of at school. He promised to return as soon as he could to give us another ride. I thought this was awful nice of him considering the circumstances.

"You've really got people talking," Hodge said. "A couple of kids discovered your blood in the hallway and got a janitor and some higher ups involved. I spoke with the deans and let them know what really happened." He looked guilty as he said this, like he was ashamed of himself for doing his duty as a professor. "I really wish that things had turned out differently. Truthfully, you two were my best students. Even you, June. Your grades weren't great, but I could tell you put in a good effort." Addressing only Pat he added, "The deans want to see you when you get back."

Pat hopped down from the table and grimaced. The nurse reprimanded him for being so careless and told him to return if the stitches came loose. We thanked her for all of her help, but her attention had shifted elsewhere. Some guy had been rolled in on a stretcher with his head dented like a can of beans. She rushed to his aid, calling out for help from anyone who would listen. We felt like we were in the way and ran out.

When we got back to school, Pat asked whether he had to report to the deans straight away, or if he could procrastinate. Professor Hodge must've really felt real bad for turning him in, because he agreed to allow him some time to himself, so long as he met up with the deans sometime that day.

The first thing Pat wanted to do was retrieve our stuff from the classroom. We were relieved to find everything just as we had left it. Even the Christmas lights were still plugged in, though now they were scorching hot. Pat bent over to fold my blanket and cried out in pain. I told him to have a seat while I cleaned everything up.

I took a good look at our cocoon before disassembling it. I figured that this would be the last time I'd see room 103 so decked out, which made me depressed. I wished that I had brought a camera with me to capture the moment forever. Well, not to capture that moment exactly, but all the ones that came before it.

As I sorted through our albums I came across the remaining stash of LSD and some pot that Pat must've been planning to chase it with.

Pat caught me looking at the drugs. "Flush them," he said.

"All of them?"

He nodded. "I've had enough of that shit."

I wasted no time in doing this. Cigarettes were bad enough without bringing other shit into the mix. I only hoped that his resolve against drugs would stick.

When I returned from the bathroom I handed some records to Pat while I took everything else. He set them on his desk and asked if we could talk. His eyes were puffy and red, but for once he didn't look lost. He just looked worn out and pensive.

I took the seat next to him. "What do you want to talk about?"

"I want you to know that you were right," he said, staring out the window. He cracked it open enough to let in the fresh air, but not so much that our voices would carry. Several people were seated at picnic tables talking to their friends, while others swung side to side in rope hammocks. We had been too distracted earlier to notice what a nice day it was. The breeze was refreshing, like a cool glass of water, so I slid closer to it.

"What was I right about?" I asked.

"Everything." His breathing became unsteady and he closed his eyes. "The night of the party they slipped something in your drink June."

"*My* drink?"

"Mhmm. I didn't know that they did, and finished it after you left. I don't know what they put in there, but whatever it was, it was strong. I tried to get out of there as soon as I realized that something was wrong with me, but they insisted that I stay..." Tears spilled onto his cheeks.

"You don't have to talk about it if you aren't ready," I said.

He shook his head. "I'll never really be ready, but I want you to know. Maybe it'll lift some of the burden off of me."

"It might," I said, encouraging him. "Take your time."

He continued. "My vision became blurred and my muscles weren't working right. It felt like I was becoming paralyzed and I thought maybe I was dying. I couldn't even hold onto the beer anymore. It just slipped out of my hands and broke into a million little pieces. I managed to limp my way to the door, but they stopped me."

"Who stopped you?"

"First Jesse then a bunch of other guys on the basketball team. They were entertained by how disoriented I was, and angry that I had denied them the chance to get at you. One of the guys suggested that they fuck me to teach me a lesson, and that was a good enough excuse for everyone. Several of them grabbed me all at once. By then my body was completely limp, so they beat me and then dragged me onto the couch. I tried to scream, but I was too drugged up. Somewhere along the line I passed out. When I woke up they were gone, and I was too shocked to sort out what had happened. I don't remember the rest of the night. I think I may have puked or something."

"Yeah, you did. You came out of the building and threw up. That's how I knew that you weren't okay. I just figured you had gotten into a fight or something." I wiped away his tears with my thumbs. "I'm so sorry they did that to you, Pat. I never should have left you. I should've—"

He brushed my hair to one side and kissed me softly.

I loved it when he did that.

"I can't pretend that I'll ever be over what happened, but I've realized one thing since then," he said. "Something that helps me feel a little better when I'm in pain."

"What?"

"I'm glad that it happened to me rather than you."

The weight of this statement settled in, startling me. If I had had my way, he never would've been there that night. I would've gone to the party alone and *I* would've been the victim. Who knows what would've happened. Would I have gotten pregnant? Would I have told Pat, who probably would've set off to kill them? What would my parents have thought of the whole thing? Would they have found out? Would they have blamed me?

Pat seemed to read my mind. "June, don't think about what could have happened. I went there that night specifically to protect you, and that's what I did. Now I just have to live with the outcome."

He pushed the window open a little more. Sun splashed across his features, making him look like an angel. In many ways, that's exactly what he was to me. My boyfriend was an angel, disguised as a chain-smoking hippie.

"Thank you for saving me," I said.

"You're welcome," he said. He glanced at the pile of our belongings and sighed. "We should probably get going. I'd rather go to the man willingly than with force."

I agreed and helped him up. "Don't you think we should tell them what happened to you?"

Pat rolled his eyes.

"I mean it. The scum balls who raped you deserve to be kicked out of college more than you do. What if they've done the same thing to other people?"

"I thought about that," he said. "But there's nothing we can do. It would be my word against theirs and no one would believe me. People don't get that guys can be raped to begin with, and even girls who obviously can be are mostly ignored or blamed. One of the performers at The Comet was raped and do you know what the police said? They said they would've done it too. I guess she was wearing cutoffs when it happened. She hung herself a month later."

"That's terrible," I said. "But maybe your case will be different. Maybe they'll believe you. Jesse can't just get away with this. I won't let him."

He gathered as much stuff as he could carry without hurting himself, and headed towards the door. "Well he's going to. And don't you dare go after Jesse or do anything stupid. I don't think I could handle it if something happened to you."

I didn't say anything so he continued. "Even if anyone believed me enough to question me, they'd ask why I didn't report it sooner, and nothing I can come up with would be a good enough reason for them."

He had a point there. When we're children and get hurt, we report it straight away, eager to have attention paid to our boo-boos. This is how people expect pain to be, even as we get older. If you don't "tattle" right away, you're automatically pegged a liar. It doesn't matter how good your rationale is. I hated that this was the way things were, but felt helpless to do anything about it. Nobody knew how to approach rape back then.

"Can you promise me something?" Pat asked as we were leaving.

"Anything."

"Can you stop nagging me to talk and getting pissed at me for smoking so much? It makes me feel like an asshole and like there's something wrong with me for not being over everything by now."

"I just want to help, that's all. And cigarettes will kill you."

"I know that, but don't think that my pain has to be yours. It's mine, and mine alone. I meant what I said a couple of months ago when I told you that my smoking and stuff has nothing to do with you. You're amazing. You're beautiful. I love you. No matter where my head is at, nothing can change that. In turn I promise to listen to you when you tell me I'm being stupid. We could've avoided this whole mess if I had done that sooner."

"I'm sorry. I'll try to stop," I promised. "And I think listening sounds like a fantastic idea. Both of us should do more of that."

☼☺☼

While Pat met with the deans in one of the buildings across the street from main campus, I paced back and forth on the sidewalk. Clouds gathered overhead, blocking out the sun that we had enjoyed earlier, causing the temperature to drop dramatically. I crossed my arms over my chest which was covered with goosebumps. I wished I knew whether or not I had time to grab a jacket.

A door swung open, and Pat came rushing out of it.

"So?" I asked, struggling to read his expression.

He tugged at the hem of his shirt. "I'm officially out of here."

"Oh," I breathed. Some part of me had really believed he would be allowed to stay. "Now what?"

"I have until Wednesday to get my affairs in order and move out." His voice was surprisingly passive, as though he were commenting on the weather.

"And your parents?"

"I haven't had a chance to tell them yet. I'll do it later."

A long stretch of silence passed between us as we pondered the imponderable. Where would he go come Wednesday? And where would this leave us?

Rain fell in heavy sheets so we ducked beneath the awning. His eyes became wet with more than the rain as we stood there hoping to catch a break. I rubbed his stubble and then tucked his hair behind his ears. I planted a kiss on his forehead and one on his nose. He closed his eyes and I planted one on each lid as well.

"We'll figure it out," I said. "We'll make it work."

He opened his eyes and attempted a smile. It was weak, but not a bad effort. "Of course we will."

Chapter 21 December 5th, 1969

Pat moved away months ago, but I still wasn't used to him being

gone. Every day that I was without him felt like someone had dug

a hole in my torso and filled it with longing. It wasn't like he was

far away. He was working as a waiter and performing at The

Comet. Pat wasn't thrilled about the latter, but Dag wouldn't allow

him to do one without the other, and he really needed the cash.

Since he could no longer live on campus, he was living with his

parents until he could afford his own place.

His parents weren't surprised that he'd gotten kicked out of

college. Actually, they were surprised that he had lasted as long as

he had on account of his "strange" beliefs. They told him that he

could live with them so long as he enlisted to serve in Vietnam after Christmas. He agreed to this arrangement, figuring that he'd have plenty of time to find a way out of it.

There were loads of methods people were using to disqualify themselves from being accepted into service, but none that he was willing to try. Slicing a thumb off would be painful, and he liked all of his appendages. He didn't have any medical ailments that he knew of, other than a touch of scoliosis. He was young, thin, and had perfect eyesight. He had mental wounds, but no psychiatric record. He was, in most people's eyes, an ideal candidate for any branch of the military.

We made it a point to see each other every Monday when he had off of work, but other than that our schedules never lined up. While I was in class, he was at home. When my day was over, his night at the restaurant was just beginning. Once and a while I convinced my roommate to come visit him with me, but we couldn't afford to do it all the time. Even if we could, sometimes she just didn't feel like going. I can't say that I blamed her. It was a long walk after all, and seeing him work didn't give her the same thrill that it gave me.

The first Friday of December was one of those rare nights when Kyoko reluctantly said yes to visiting Pat. It was the type of night that it didn't matter how many layers we wore; Jack Frost found a way through them all. By the time we made it to the restaurant we were both so cold that we had headaches. We quickly said "hello" to the woman behind the hostess's podium, who sat us at the table furthest from the door.

There were two older women at the booth diagonal from us. One lit a cigarette while the other went over to the bar to order a gin and tonic. The one at the booth yawned and reached into her purse for her compact mirror. She pulled it out and powdered her face, then applied a thick layer of burgundy lipstick.

Pat emerged from the kitchen with two plates in his hands and another balanced on his forearm. The woman ignored him as he served them their food, and called her friend over to eat. His forearm was bright red from where the hot plate had pressed against his skin, but he didn't seem to notice. He scanned the restaurant for other customers then came over to our table.

"Hey," he said, drawing together his brows. "What're you doing here?"

"Visiting you," I smiled.

He didn't smile back.

"Shouldn't we have?"

He lowered his chin and asked us what we wanted to drink.

Pat *never* asked us what we wanted to drink. Usually he just

brought us two ice teas and a bonus: spicy nachos when it was

freezing or a basket of fries when the weather was tolerable.

"Uh, I could go for some tea and nachos," I said. Turning

to my roommate I added, "What about you Kyoko?"

"That sounds good," she said.

He tore off a piece of his notepad which he hadn't written

anything on, and went into the kitchen.

"What's gotten into him?" Kyoko asked.

"I have no idea."

We quietly chatted while we waited for our beverages. It

took Pat a full fifteen minutes to return. When he did, his hands

were trembling so hard that he dropped one of the glasses and it

landed with a dramatic crash. Shards flew across the floor and

under our table. I kicked them into a small pile, while Pat stared down at them. He cupped his hands over his ears, swaying his head from side to side.

The women at the booth next to us commented that he was a fucking klutz. A coworker offered him a broom and a dustpan. Pat stood there, frozen, taking none of it in.

I recognized his symptoms, and knew he was on the verge of an episode.

"I could really use some fresh air," I said to him. "Got a few minutes to take a break?"

His expression grew even more vacant.

"Hey, Pat" I said, slightly louder than before. I knelt down so that I was in his line of vision, but not so close that we touched. I had learned not to touch him while he was like this. One touch and he'd flip shit. He wasn't himself when the trauma took over; he couldn't help it.

He blinked several times, and began breathing slowly, carefully.

"Can you come outside with me?" I asked.

He nodded. "Yeah, let's go."

My roommate looked worried, but busied herself with her napkin. She folded and unfolded it, as though it were origami. His coworker looked pissed, but swept up the glass.

Outside Pat lit a cigarette and leaned against the front window. I gazed past him at my roommate who was watching us like we were the leads on a soap. I waved her off. She began rearranging the salt and pepper shakers on the table.

"I've been drafted," Pat said.

"You've...what?"

"Didn't you watch the draft the other night?"

I shook my head. My professor had mentioned something about it, but I didn't think that it pertained to anyone I knew. Instead I had taken advantage of the empty dormitory by taking my first warm shower in weeks. I loved when everyone else was away.

"Oh, I thought you would have," he said. "Since I'm not in school anymore, I wasn't exempt."

"I didn't know that," I said. "I'm sorry."

"The first date that they pulled was my birthday. Can you believe it? September 14th. My fucking luck. I broke down right then and there, but my old man said to toughen up. He was the one who made the draft board aware of my change of status when I got kicked out of college. He said he is proud that I'm going off to fight for the American way." He spat on the sidewalk, "Who's way is that anyway?"

My stomach collapsed into itself. I wasn't ready for this. I knew that in a few weeks his parents expected him to enlist, but I never thought it would actually happen. It wasn't fair. They couldn't make him fight in a war that he didn't believe in. A war that he was likely to die in if not return more broken than he already was. Whose parents in their right mind would support such a thing?

"There has to be a way out," I said, quickly glancing inside the restaurant. Kyoko had grown bored with organizing the spices and was staring at us again. This time I didn't bother to wave her off. I'd tell her everything later on anyway.

Pat drew himself upward. "I'll try to think of something," he said. "I go for my physical exam in less than a week. That's when I'll know for sure if I'm going. Until then, can you pray for me?"

"*Pray* for you?"

"Yeah, you heard me. If there *is* a dictator in the sky, I want them to look out for me. I figure you have better pull with them than I do." He opened the door for me and I went inside. He served us our nachos like nothing had happened, and I filled Kyoko in when he wasn't around. She took the news badly, as though he were her own boyfriend. I warned her to remain cool; I didn't want Pat getting upset again.

I snuck Pat a kiss when we were finished eating, and placed a hefty tip on the table. It didn't really matter how much I left him because he insisted on paying for all our dates, but it made me feel better. Kyoko was generous too, leaving ten percent too much.

We walked back to the school in silence, sleet stinging our faces. When we arrived at our dorm, I hesitated to produce the key. Kyoko rooted through her clutch and eventually found hers. She stuck it into the door, and twisted it open.

"You coming?" she asked, shedding her coat and scarf.

"I'll catch up with you later," I said. "There's something I want to do."

"Suit yourself," she said, tossing the scarf to me. It smelled like citrus and lilies. "Try not to freeze to death."

☼☺☼

When I arrived at the chapel, it was empty and dark. I turned on the lights and sat in the front pew. The bench was too hard for my bony ass, so I stood up and moved to the side of the room. Beneath the windows were shelves lined with fat beeswax candles, and cups containing long matchsticks. I used one of the sticks to light every candle, and then got down on my hands and knees to pray.

"Hey God," I said. "Long time no talk. Sorry about that." My palms became sweaty and stuck to the floor. I lifted them and they were caked with dust and stray hairs. I wiped them against my jeans, but it didn't help remove the grime. The hairs only got tangled around my fingers.

I continued, "I know you and I haven't exactly been close lately, but can you do me a favor? My boyfriend, Pat, he's a really great guy." I closed my eyes, picturing Pat and recalling all of the amazing things he had done.

"Please save him, God. He's too fragile for war. There's no way he'll survive. Not on the battlefield and not at home if he makes it that far. Please. If you're up there, you have to do something. I'm doing all I can down here, and so is he. It's your turn. I trust you. *We* trust you... in our own way."

I crossed my head and my heart and kissed the dirty floor. I stood up and blew out the candles one by one, allowing my worries to melt right along with the beeswax. Now all that was left to do was wait.

Chapter 22: December 12th, 1969

The day before winter break, I opened my eyes to find a sheet of lined paper taped to my forehead. I sat up, unstuck it, and looked over at Kyoko who was packing. She would be flying home to Japan in a couple of hours, but you wouldn't have known it by her lack of preparation. Sweaters and skirts were strewn all over the floor, and her plane ticket was crumpled on her desk next to a rotten apple.

"*Really*?" I asked, waving the note at her.

"I didn't write that," she said. "Did you even read it?"

I unfolded it carefully, but still managed to tear the corner. It read, "Meet me in Parker Hall: ASAP."

"Oh no," I said, jumping out of bed. "This can't be good."

"What?" she asked concerned.

"I think it's from Pat. He must've had his army physical."

"Well you better get going then," she said. "Don't make him wait all day."

I put on my patched jacket and traded my pajama bottoms for jeans. I quickly brushed my teeth and hair and did all of the other things required to make myself look presentable. I wanted to respect his request to get there soon, but if this was the last time that I'd see him for a while—or ever—I wanted to look good.

I said goodbye to Kyoko who beamed at me as I left. I wondered what she was so happy about then assumed she was just looking forward to break. We all needed time off from the demands of college life, and sophomore year was proving to be academically challenging. Neither one of us had managed to make it onto the dean's list, despite the fact that we had been studying harder than ever. Even changing my major to art hadn't increased my GPA, but at least I enjoyed my classes.

Most students had gone home already, so Parker Hall was a ghost town. My boots squeaked as I walked so with every step I heard, "Save-Pat, Save-Pat, Save-Pat." I glanced up at the ceiling and it was the first time that I noticed a paper star hanging overhead. I wondered if it was new, or if it'd been there all along.

Inside of room 103 the overhead lights were off but the room was glowing. Multi-colored Christmas lights were strung between the desks and along the window frames. The desks neatly lined both sides of the room, and a strip of emerald fabric was placed between them. Strewn on it were rose petals whose perfume permeated the air, and lush branches of pine.

At the far end of the display stood Pat, who grinned as I entered. He switched on his turntable and placed the needle on the album. It spun several times then "And I Love Her" began to play. He had adjusted the speed so that it was slightly slower than usual, making it sound slightly creepy, but also romantic.

"What's all this?" I asked, approaching him.

He was wearing my favorite vest of his; a tan one that was softer than a baby's butt. He smelled like cigarettes and earthy cologne, the latter of which was rare. I reached out to hug him, but he knelt down in front of me. He pulled out a sheer pouch and undid its drawstrings. Inside was a citrine daisy ring with a shiny gold band.

He held it out to me and said, "We've been going out a year now and we've been through hell. It's made me realize how crazy life can be and how quickly things can change. But there are some things that I don't want to change, like you and me. You're the only one who really gets me, and I never want to lose you. Will you marry me?"

I looked behind him at a poster of Uncle Sam tacked onto the wall. It reminded me of the war that was still raging on the other side of the world. A war that Pat would soon be forced to fight in against his will.

Of course, I thought. Pat, like so many others, wanted to wed before being shipped off to his grave. I wondered how long we'd have together before this happened. Months? Weeks? Days?

Would I have time to make a dress? Would we have to be wed at the courthouse?

"Yes," I said. "I can't imagine my life without you either. But so help me God, you better not get into drugs again. I want to be sure that I'm marrying *you*. Not them."

"I'll try not to," he said seriously. "But if I do you have every right to leave me."

I held out my hand and he slid the ring onto my finger. It was nontraditional, to be sure, and my mother would be horrified by it. But it was also the most beautiful thing I had ever seen, even beating the view on our Valentine's Day.

Married. *Married*. I was going to be somebody's wife after all. It was a role I had always been unsure about, a role that I had never aspired to, yet wanted more than anything. Now it made sense in the context of my life. *Married*.

"Do you like the ring?" he asked, interrupting my thoughts. "If not we can return it and you can pick out your own."

"You couldn't have picked a more perfect one," I said. This was more than true.

I held it up to the Christmas lights to admire it again. Inscribed on the inside was "08/24/1968". The day that for Pat had been love at first sight. The day that I knew we had something special.

"So when do you leave?" I asked. I didn't want shit on our happiness, but I needed to know how much longer we'd have together.

"For what?" he asked.

"Vietnam."

"Oh." He wrapped his arms around me, massaging my stomach with his fingers. "Never."

My mouth fell open. "You're not going?"

"Nope."

"How is that possible?" I instinctively began inspecting his body. It looked like all of his appendages were still in tact, and he didn't suffer from any diseases that I knew of. He had gained a little weight since getting kicked out of school, and some muscle mass from lifting trays at The Comet. If anything, he was more suited than ever to go off to war.

"Let's just say that I failed my physical exam," he said.

272

"You're going to have to give me a little more than that."

His eyes became squinty from how wide his smile was. He bit his lips to avoid laughing. "Have you noticed that you're missing your indigo pair of panties? You know, the real pretty ones with the lace trim?"

I thought about it. "Yeah I guess so. Why?"

"I wore them to the exam."

"You didn't."

He nodded. "I wish you could've been there. I just as soon pulled down my pants as they told me to get the hell out of there. They looked legitimately scared of me, and several men whistled and called me a fairy on the way out."

"That's horrible."

"It is...but it worked."

We couldn't contain ourselves. Our bodies shook from laughter, from joy, from pure relief. They shook so hard that our ribs felt broken, and eventually we began to cry.

Pat had worn my panties to get out of going to war, and I couldn't have been more relieved. I imagined the horrified looks on the faces of everyone on the draft board. They were local guys, like my father, who would peg him a traitor and a coward for pulling such a stunt, if only they could be sure that it wasn't a regular occurrence. They'd say he was un-American and disrespecting all those who had previously served. But this wasn't about previous wars. And it wasn't a matter of respect. Put simply, Pat felt he was doing the right thing.

"I don't think I've ever been this happy before," he said once we'd settled down. "Of course, my parents are pissed at me. I told them I was rejected because of asthma. They knew I was lying, and my dad whipped me with his belt like he did when I was a kid. It may be a few years before they speak to me again, but I'm okay with that. I have you."

"That you do," I said, reaching for his hand. I'd have to get used to the feeling of the engagement ring gently pinching my skin as our fingers interlocked. "My mom won't be happy when she finds out we're getting married," I said. "Every time I call she asks whether we've broken up yet."

"I never knew that," he said.

"She asks every single time."

His face fell. "Are you alright with that? I mean, I know how much your folks mean to you."

I opened my mouth to respond yes, but then closed it. *Was* I okay marrying someone she didn't approve of? It was true that my mom annoyed me to no end, but what Pat said was also true. My folks meant a lot to me, despite our differences. I worried that by straying too far beyond their velvet leash I'd eventually be cut off.

Then there was Pat, the person I loved more than anyone. It was true that he wasn't perfect, but then again, neither was I. He still smoked when his mind veered into dark places, and had episodes every now and then. I still struggled not to take his behaviors personally, and was learning to be okay with giving him space when he needed it. But we were working through our problems together, figuring out his triggers and talking openly about how we felt. I truly believed that regardless of our past, Pat and I would have a good future together. In many ways our relationship was stronger because of what happened.

When I spoke this time, I was sure that what I was about to say was the absolute truth. "If they don't accept you as family, then they're no longer mine. A true Christian would let God do the judging and stick to being nice. I'll remind them of that and see how it goes."

He stroked the ring on my finger. "Probably not great," he said. "Let's just hope they don't hear about my army physical. That would really do them in."

The music stopped playing, so Pat put on another album. The record played smoothly, no pennies required. He invited me to dance and we did, like the two uncoordinated hippies we were. He spun me around in circles until I could no longer stand upright. I tried to dip him like I'd seen professionals do on TV, and we both collapsed onto the floor.

The song "Go Where you Wanna Go" finished, and the record stopped spinning. We laid there holding hands, just enjoying each other's company.

"So what's next?" Pat asked, grinning sideways at me. "We could lie here the rest of the weekend, or until Hodge kicks us out. We could run off and get married, just the two of us and the JP. We could...well I don't know June. What do you want to do?"

I tucked his hair behind his ears and kissed his stubbly cheek. "Everything is an option," I said. *"Everything."*

ABOUT PAIGE HAWK

Paige received her Bachelor's degree in Marketing Communications from Moravian College. It was here that she was inspired to write *The Wounds That Don't Bleed*, after becoming fascinated by a photo in their archives. Described as a flower child by her friends, it is Paige's dream to promote a better world through writing.

Find out more about Paige at www.PaigeEHawk.weebly.com

Made in the USA
Middletown, DE
12 November 2019

78247021R10172